"I want to give you a magic place, where nothing can ever go wrong, Damita," Cam said softly. *"A place where your feet don't have to touch the ground, and you can wander with someone who loves you."*

Damita inhaled sharply. Cam's gaze was holding her with the seductive power of a caress. She could see the rapid pulse in his temple and his lips were no longer smiling but heavy with sensuality. She was suddenly conscious of the textures of her body, the fullness of her breasts, the blood pounding in her veins.

"Damita." He reached across the table and touched her hand. It was a casual caress but her reaction to it was anything but. She began to tremble. The warmth of his flesh, the masculine hardness of his hand struck her with a force that stunned her. Waves of heat began to sweep through her body. Suddenly warmth and safety were gone, and there was only this need, only heat and hunger and power drawing her toward him. . . .

WHAT ARE *LOVESWEPT* ROMANCES?

They are stories of true romance and touching emotion. We believe those two very important ingredients are constants in our highly sensual and very believable stories in the *LOVESWEPT* line. Our goal is to give you, the reader, stories of consistently high quality that may sometimes make you laugh, sometimes make you cry, but are always fresh and creative and contain many delightful surprises within their pages.

Most romance fans read an enormous number of books. Those they truly love, they keep. Others may be traded with friends and soon forgotten. We hope that each *LOVESWEPT* romance will be a treasure—a "keeper." We will always try to publish

LOVE STORIES YOU'LL NEVER FORGET
BY AUTHORS YOU'LL ALWAYS REMEMBER

The Editors

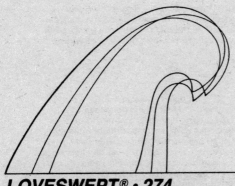

LOVESWEPT® • 274

Iris Johansen
Blue Skies and Shining Promises

 BANTAM BOOKS
TORONTO • NEW YORK • LONDON • SYDNEY • AUCKLAND

BLUE SKIES AND SHINING PROMISES

A Bantam Book / August 1988

If you would be interested in receiving protective vinyl
covers for your Loveswept books, please write to this address
for information:

Loveswept
Bantam Books
P.O. Box 985
Hicksville, NY 11802

ISBN 0-553-21915-4

One

Damita wrinkled her nose, trying to ward off a sneeze. Blast the idiotic veil she wore. How could Moslem women tolerate them? They were uncomfortable as the devil and seemed at every turn to trap dust motes that tickled her nose and made her eyes water. But she knew she really shouldn't criticize the veil, at least not now, because it caused all the chambermaids to look like clones of one another, and that made her scheme workable.

But still she scowled as she chalked one more score against Cameron Bandor's growing account. Only a flamboyant sexist would force the maids in his hotel to wear these exotic outfits just to provide atmosphere for his guests.

She adjusted the dark blue veiling covering her face and headed across a lobby that bore a distinct resemblance to a Turkish seraglio to the reception desk. She was forced to detour around a roaring vacuum cleaner wielded by a porter before reaching the desk clerk, who gazed at her with disinterest before covering his lips to smother a yawn.

Damita boldly went behind the desk and reached for the key in the slot labeled CB. "Mrs. Kalim needs a key for Mr. Bandor's suite. One of the new maids misplaced the master key and he called down to housekeeping for fresh towels."

The clerk yawned again. "Be sure to bring it back before I go off duty."

"I will," she promised in a voice kept carefully casual. She turned in a whirl of sheer draperies, walking quickly from behind the desk and across the lobby to the service elevator. She pressed the button for the penthouse and breathed a sigh of relief as the elevator doors closed, enfolding her in momentary security. That hadn't been so difficult. It had been much harder to do the preliminary scouting to find out the name of the hotel housekeeper and obtain this haremlike uniform. She had thought if she timed her invasion of Bandor's suite for four o'clock in the morning it would have a reasonable chance of success. Everything was always more lax in this period between night and dawn.

She gripped the key tightly as the elevator door opened. She mustn't lose her nerve now. Hesitating only an instant, she stepped into the lushly carpeted hallway to confront a set of elaborately carved double doors, the portal to Bandor's suite that was said to take up the entire floor. Appropriate, she thought disparagingly, that these lavish doors were as ostentatious as the rest of the Marasef Bandor Hotel. She used the key and stepped into the dark foyer of the suite. How could Lola have become involved with a man like Bandor? She usually chose lovers who were discriminating and sophisticated and, if his hotel were any indication, Bandor was totally lacking in both qualities.

Well, she wasn't here to criticize Lola's taste in men, she thought, but to obtain information, and she'd best set about doing it. She braced herself and briskly crossed the sitting room and threw open the door. "Mr. Bandor, I have to talk to you," she announced loudly, simultaneously switching on the overhead light. "I'm sorry to disturb you at this hour, but it's entirely your own fault for not—" She broke off. "Oh, I didn't realize you were . . . busy."

The blonde lying beside the man in the king-size bed rose up on one elbow to gaze at her with drowsy indignation. "Cam, who is this woman?"

"I have no idea." Cameron Bandor sat up in bed, the sheet falling to his waist to bare a broad chest thatched with springy dark hair. "But I believe I'd better find out." His gaze was remarkably wide awake as it slowly raked Damita's veiled figure, lingering on the fullness of her breasts in the skimpy gold-embroidered jacket. "I take it you're one of my employees? If you've chosen this opportunity to hit me for a raise, your timing is abominable, luv." His drawl was lazy, the words faintly flavored with an Australian accent, and he appeared neither angry nor disconcerted. The deep blue eyes studying her held only interest and curiosity. "But I do applaud your initiative."

Damita frowned. "I don't work for you." She slammed the door behind her and moved across the room toward the bed. "I've been trying for three days to see you, but those watchdogs downstairs wouldn't even let me call you on the house phone. You'd think I was trying to assassinate you or something."

"I've been in conference with my architects," he said absently. "You have truly magnificent eyes. Would you mind removing that veil?"

Damita jerked the veil away from her face. "These veils are very uncomfortable, you know. You shouldn't force your maids to bundle up in them." She wrinkled her nose distastefully. "I don't know why they put up with it."

"Money. I pay them extraordinarily well to fulfill the Arabian Nights fantasies of our guests." His gaze searched her face intently. "But I'm sorry if it inconvenienced you."

The blonde stirred restlessly. "Send her away, Cam. I want to go back to sleep."

Bandor's gaze didn't leave Damita's face. "Now, we mustn't be inhospitable, Myra. Life can be very dull without little diversions."

Damita plopped down in the chair beside the bed. "We could do better without her here. Since you just woke up, surely you've finished—" She paused. "I mean, I need to talk to you."

Bandor's eyes twinkled. "Didn't anyone ever tell you it's rude to kiss and run?"

"It's only sex," Damita said impatiently. "Couldn't you tell her to come back later?"

"Only?" Bandor studied Damita for a moment and then turned to the blonde and smiled faintly. "Run along, Myra. I'll call you this afternoon."

"But I don't—" The blonde broke off as she took in Bandor's expression. She reluctantly sat up, slipped on a robe that Bandor had retrieved from the foot of the bed and handed to her, then got up. She scowled at Damita and stalked into the bathroom, slamming the door.

"Now." His gaze returned to Damita. "Would you like to begin our discussion or would you like to take her place?"

She blinked. "I beg your pardon?"

He sighed. "You really do want to talk. Pity. I half hoped you were lusting after my body." He threw aside the sheet, got out of bed, and strolled toward the closet in splendid and unashamed nudity. "You obviously know who I am, but I haven't had the honor of being introduced. Am I to be permitted to know your name?"

"What?" He wasn't at all what she had expected, she thought. His reaction to her intrusion was

. . . unusual. He seemed to accept her sudden appearance with only zestful good humor and curiosity.

He glanced over his shoulder as he reached for a crimson velour robe. "Your name?"

"Oh, Damita. Damita Shaughnessy." Lord, the man was sexy, she thought with an odd quivery sensation in the pit of her stomach. Now she could easily understand why Lola had become involved with him. No one could say Lola wasn't vulnerable to sex appeal.

Bandor's tobacco-brown hair was flecked with silver at the temples, but she judged him to be only in his mid-thirties. His high cheekbones and well-shaped lips were sculpted perfection, and the expression in those deep blue eyes alternated between beguiling mischief and steamy sensuality. He appeared to be just under six feet tall; his body was as sinewy and tough-looking as that of a young stallion. The muscles of his buttocks rippled as he shifted to slip into his robe, and Damita forced her gaze away from him. She was breathless, she realized in surprise, and her cheeks felt suddenly hot. How stupid. Male nudity was no oddity to her. Why did seeing Bandor's body have this effect?

"Damita Shaughnessy." He was turning to face her. "That's an unusual combination. Spanish and Irish." He crossed the room and sat down on the edge of the bed, tilting his head to study her. "You don't look Irish. The Spanish part is obvious enough; those big dark eyes are practically Madonna-like." He reached out and pushed back the veil covering her head until it fell to her shoulders to reveal her short red hair. He smiled with satisfaction as if he'd made a great discovery. "Ah, there's the Irish. I've always liked redheads."

The color deepened in her cheeks. "From the newspaper articles I've read, it appears you like women, period."

He nodded. "I do like women. I find them endlessly fascinating."

"In bed," she added crisply.

"Oh, yes. Definitely in bed. But elsewhere too. Sorry to disillusion you, but I don't regard women as sexual toys. Playmates but not toys."

She nodded jerkily toward the bathroom into which the blonde had disappeared. "Even that Bo Derek lookalike?"

"Myra? I gave her what she wanted and she gave me what I needed," he said simply. "Myra doesn't want anything else from me, and I assure you she doesn't feel used."

The lady in question burst out of the bathroom, now dressed in elegant slacks and a silk blouse. She gave Damita another cutting glance before crossing the room and dropping a kiss on Bandor's temple. Her face softened miraculously as she looked down at him. "Call me." She whirled and strode out of the room, slamming the door behind her.

Damita stared after her in puzzlement. It was

clear the woman felt no resentment toward Bandor, even though she had been summarily dismissed. In fact, she seemed only to have great affection for him. How very odd. Damita forced her attention back to more important issues. "Your personal affairs don't interest me, Mr. Bandor."

He lifted his brow. "Really? That's too bad. Your personal affairs interest me very much indeed. Are you married?"

"No." She frowned. "That's none of your business."

He chuckled. "I think I'm entitled to a few facts about you. It's not every day a woman forces her way into my suite and insists I send away—"

"I didn't force my way in," Damita interrupted indignantly. "I used a key."

"Obviously obtained by nefarious means." He shook his head. "It's much the same thing, luv."

"Well, it wouldn't have been necessary if you'd consented to see me. I told you why I was forced to do this. Just tell me what I want to know and I'll leave you alone."

"But I'm not sure I want you to leave me alone," he said calmly. "Nothing this interesting has happened to me in a long time. I've always been of the philosophy that one should never let an intriguing possibility pass until one has explored every facet of it." His voice lowered to soft seduction. "Are you sure you don't want to come to bed with me? It's an excellent method of exploration and discovery."

"I'm sure," she said curtly. "After I've gone you can phone down for your friend, Myra."

He slowly shook his head. "I don't think so. I'm more selective than you might believe from the circumstances. Sometimes sex is enough, but I don't believe it will suffice in your case."

"Look, will you be serious?" She leaned forward in the chair. "I know that this is some kind of line and you're not really attracted to me. I have one question to ask and then I'll get out of your life. Where is Lola Torres?"

He went still. "Why do you want to know?"

"I have to find her."

His gaze was wary. "Why come to me?"

"Because you were her lover," Damita said bluntly. "The newspapers were full of innuendos about the two of you, and she spent two months here at your hotel in Marasef."

"The paparazzi are seldom accurate about anything." His accent no longer sounded lazy, but hard and clipped. "Lola has a certain notoriety—"

"And you don't?" Damita's eyes were blazing. "That's rather like the pot calling the kettle black, isn't it? According to the stories I've heard, Casanova was a monk compared to you. Clean up your own act before you cast stones at Lola."

"I'm not casting stones." His gaze narrowed on her face. "You're very defensive. Are you really a friend of Lola's?"

"You're damn right I am." Her hands closed tightly on the arms of the chair. "Lola and I are very close and I'm worried about her. After she left Marasef, it was as if she fell off the edge of the earth."

"And here there be dragons," he said softly.

"What?"

"On some old maps those words were written in the seas. I often wondered how the seamen felt sailing toward the horizon where that fate awaited."

"But there weren't any dragons waiting there," she said impatiently. "And what does that nonsense have to do with Lola anyway?"

"Dragons come in many guises. You can't be sure that one isn't waiting at the most seemingly innocuous place."

He was rather like a great bronzed dragon himself at that moment, tranquil on the surface, yet darkly dangerous, she thought with a shiver. He had changed from a charming rogue into a menacing man in the space of a heartbeat. The room seemed to grow smaller, and she was abruptly conscious of how alone they were. What did she really know about Cameron Bandor? The newspaper accounts regarding his past had been very scanty, reporters apparently preferring to concentrate on his very colorful present. He was rumored to be half Sedikhanese and half Swiss and had appeared on the world economic scene some years ago when he and his stepbrother, Jordan, had opened a chain of luxury hotels that rivaled the Hiltons. Every hotel took its theme from the city or country in which it resided and the tourists had become enamored with both the hotels' luxurious efficiency and the blatantly exotic atmosphere assured them at each location. He was undoubtedly wealthy, intelligent, and charismatic, but now there seemed to be a good deal beneath his charming facade that journalists had not been able to fathom. *Here there be dragons.* . . . "Are you threatening me?"

"No," he said softly. "I was wondering if you were a threat to me. Are you?"

"Of course not. I'm not a threat to anyone. If you'll only tell me where Lola is right now I'll—"

"Why are you so certain that I know?"

"I wasn't, until you started hemming and hawing," Damita said bluntly. "I hoped you might know something but I wasn't sure." She paused. "Now I am. You do know where Lola is, don't you, Mr. Bandor?"

"Perhaps." His gaze was fixed on her face. "Lola moves around quite a bit. Marasef one month, Cannes the next—"

"But never without letting me know," Damita burst out. "She would have told me—" She stopped and tried to steady her voice. "Lola and I are very close. She never let a week go by without writing or phoning me, and I haven't heard from her in over two months."

His lips twisted in a skeptical smile. "You'll forgive me if I find that hard to believe. Lola and I became quite good friends while she was here and she never mentioned your name in all that time."

"She never mentions me to anyone," Damita said. "It doesn't matter how fond she was of you, she still wouldn't have mentioned me."

"Why?"

"It doesn't matter. It has nothing to do with you." She expelled her breath in a burst of exasperation. "Why are you acting like this? You'd think I was a criminal or something."

"The notion did occur to me." Then, as she gazed at him in bewilderment, a faint smile touched his lips. "But I'm beginning to change my mind. You'd have to be a consummate actress of the Meryl Streep caliber to appear this transparent."

"Transparent?" She wasn't sure she liked that description. "If you mean I believe in being honest and straightforward, then you're right. I've never had any use for lies." Her tone had a sudden passion. "I hate deception."

"And yet I detect a certain evasiveness." He met her gaze. "Don't I, Damita Shaughnessy?"

She gazed at him, helpless and frustrated. "You *do* know where she is. Why won't you tell me? Is there something wrong with her?" Sudden fear darkened her eyes. "She's not ill?"

"She was hale and hearty the last time I saw her."

"That's no real answer."

He rose to his feet. "That's all you're going to get from me at present. You're an unknown quantity, Damita, and I'm not exactly a trusting bloke. I don't like evasion."

"But you don't understand—" She stopped. His expression was unrelenting. "Lola's in trouble, isn't she?"

"Let's say she could be in a better situation."

"Then I should be with her. Don't you see?" But how could he see? she thought desperately. Bandor was a hard man, and the expression in those blue eyes was definitely skeptical. There was no way out. She'd have to tell him. She drew a deep breath and then said in a little rush, "Lola Torres is my mother."

Surprise flickered in his face. "I find that difficult to believe."

"I know I don't look anything like Lola, but it's true." Her hands clenched nervously in her lap. "Oh, damn, Lola is going to kill me. She made me promise I'd never tell anyone." She glared at him. "If you'd been willing to cooperate, I wouldn't have had to break my word."

"Sorry, I'll try to do better in future." The words were absent as his gaze searched her face. "You could be related. Your eyes are a little like Lola's, but—"

"But I'm not a world-famous beauty. I'm not tall and voluptuous. I'm short, plump, and your average garden-variety woman." Her tone was completely free of bitterness. "Even sex goddesses are capable of having quite ordinary children."

"I'd never refer to you as ordinary," he murmured.

She shook her head and her short flyaway curls glinted with dark fire as they caught the light. "You don't have to be kind to me. I know exactly who and what I am. I have my feet planted on the ground and I learned a long time ago that I'd never have the kind of appeal Lola has."

"How very sensible of you." His gaze lingered on the strong planes of her face before moving down to the soft vulnerability of her lips. "Your face has character but it's true you're no conventional beauty, Damita."

Damita felt a tiny shock and then a strange pang that might have been hurt. Bandor evidently wasn't a man who minced words. "Will you please tell me where I can find Lola? Surely you can see her own daughter would never do anything to hurt her."

"You've obviously never read *Mommie Dearest*. Mother-daughter relationships aren't always warm and wonderful. I find it very curious that no one has ever heard of Lola having a daughter."

"I told you, Lola didn't want anyone to know about me."

"Why not? Lola is one of the most frank and honest women I've ever met. Her life is an open book." He smiled faintly. "And speaking of book, no woman who wrote a book like *Kiss and Tell* would be embarrassed about disclosing the fact that she'd had a child in or out of wedlock. It won't wash, Damita."

"But don't you understand?" She jumped to her

feet and took an impulsive step toward him, her dark eyes glittering with tears. "It was for *me*. She didn't want to let anyone know she was my mother because she was afraid I'd be hurt. That people would say like mother, like daughter. She wanted to keep me safe." She moistened her lips with her tongue. "When I was old enough to realize who she was and what she had done, I tried to tell her that I didn't care what people thought. But she wouldn't listen. She made me promise that I'd never reveal to anyone that she was my mother."

"You're obviously in your twenties. Lola is too young to have—"

"I'm twenty-three and Lola was fourteen when I was born." She paused. "What do you know about my mother?"

He hesitated. "I thought I knew her very well, but I'm beginning to believe I was mistaken. She never actually spoke about her past; I suppose I know only what everybody else knows—that she was a high-priced call girl who wrote an exposé on the sexual secrets of her famous lovers. Later she became a personality on the talk show circuit. She appears to have plenty of money and a number of very powerful 'friends.' "

"Including you." Damita smiled bitterly. "No one seems to wonder *why* Lola became a call girl or wrote that book. Did you know that she was the daughter of a prostitute and a drug runner, that she lived in the barrios of Los Angeles and went through experiences that would have destroyed anyone who didn't have a streak of stainless steel? She ran wild in the streets from the time she was nine and was pregnant by the time she was thirteen. She gave birth to me in a rat-infested tenement with only a midwife to help her because she was afraid the welfare people would take me away from her. Did you know all that?"

"No. No I didn't."

"Well, she did," Damita said fiercely. "And then she went out and earned money to support us in the only way an uneducated teenage girl in the barrios could. She's damned wonderful."

"I agree," he said gently. "You're preaching to the converted, Damita."

Damita rushed on as if he hadn't spoken. "She sent me to a convent in Mexico when I was three, but she visited me whenever she could. And she sent me to college and gave me everything any girl could want. She's my mother and my best friend and—"

"Hush, Damita." Bandor placed two fingers on her lips, silencing the feverish flow of words. "Don't be so defensive. I'm not attacking Lola. We all fight with whatever weapons we're given. Lola was given strength, an intelligent mind, and a beautiful body. Naturally, she used all of them to get out of the barrios and make a life for both of you."

A current of warmth radiated through her. "You don't condemn her?"

His lips twisted. "Lord, no. Why should I? She's

a damn fine woman. I haven't led a blameless life myself."

"So I've heard," she said dryly. "Well, I won't keep you any longer. If you'll just tell me where I can find my mother, I promise I won't bother you again."

"You won't? That's disappointing." He turned away. "I'll call downstairs and arrange for you to be given a suite and send someone to have your belongings packed and sent over. Where are you staying?"

"The Sheraton," she answered automatically. "But what are you talking about? I'm not going to stay here. I'll probably leave Sedikhan as soon as you tell me—"

"But I have no intention of telling you anything." He added softly, "Yet. It's entirely possible you're lying to me and I don't put my friends in jeopardy without proof. No, it's too risky. I've got to check your story out before I reunite you with Lola."

"And how do you intend to do that?"

He smiled. "Why, through Lola herself. I'll contact her and ask a few questions about you. In the meantime, I want you where I can keep my eye on you."

She frowned. "Why?"

His smile deepened, but she was aware of sudden chilling menace. "So that I can break that soft pretty neck if I find out you're not who you say you are. I don't like being used."

Damita's eyes widened. "But I'm telling you the truth."

"We'll see." He rose and picked up the receiver from the phone on the teak nightstand. "It shouldn't take more than a few days to check."

"A few days," Damita echoed. "Why should it take that long if you're going to phone her?"

He looked down at the phone and punched in a number. "Lola's out of touch at present."

Damita felt a wave of panic rush through her. "But she's all right? You said nothing was wrong."

He looked up. "She's fine. Just—"

"Out of touch," Damita finished tartly. "You're being annoyingly mysterious."

"Mysteries may be annoying but they're always interesting. What would life be without them?" Someone answered on the other end of the phone and Bandor gave quick, incisive instructions to the desk clerk before returning the receiver to its cradle. "There. A bellboy will be up to take you to your room in a few minutes." He smiled. "Unless you'd care to stay here. The offer is still open."

Damita experienced a ripple of shock. They had progressed far beyond that half-mocking invitation, and its sudden repetition confused her. "I wish you wouldn't joke," she said haltingly. "I find the idea of sharing a lover with my mother extremely distasteful."

"Do you now?" He took a step forward and touched her cheek with his index finger. "I'll have to remember that." His finger traced a path to the corner of her lips. "You're obviously a woman with firm convictions. Do you have any other prejudices?"

The warmth of his body seemed to reach out and touch her as his finger was doing. His crimson robe was only loosely tied and the edges had parted to reveal the tight curly hair feathering his chest. He was all male, bronze, tough, and virile. She had a sudden urge to lean toward him, to be drawn within the dark, warm circle of sensuality he was exuding.

Dear heaven, what was happening to her? He might be one of the sexiest men she had ever met, but he had belonged to Lola. For all she knew, he might still be her mother's lover.

She took a step back from him. "You seem to think I'm amusing."

"Oh, not amusing. Intriguing. I told you that mysteries fascinate me. I think there's more beyond that prickly surface than anyone would believe. I've never known a woman raised in a convent before." His lips twitched. "Good Lord, I think I may actually be feeling protective."

"I don't need anyone's protection. I may have grown up in a convent, but I've hardly been sheltered since then. Last week I was the only woman living with two hundred and fifty men, and I had no problem."

He lifted a brow. "Indeed? Did they take numbers?"

Her eyes were suddenly blazing. "Like mother,

like daughter? Your mind's in the sewer. No wonder Lola left—"

"*Be quiet.*" The words were enunciated with an edge of steel. There was no longer any amusement in his face. "I was joking, for heaven's sake. I know you're not a whore. It appears you're as sensitive as Lola on the subject of her past."

"I'm not! I just—" She broke off. She was trembling, she realized with amazement. Perhaps Bandor's words could hold an element of truth. She drew a shaky breath and closed her eyes. "This hasn't been an easy night for me."

"I know." His tone held such velvet tenderness that her eyes opened in surprise. She saw then the same tenderness in the expression on his face. "But it's almost over now. You've done well, Damita."

"I have?" Such simple words to bring this glowing contentment. Yet weren't these words the ones everyone wanted to hear? You've done well. You have worth and are valued.

He nodded. "You've been brave as a lion. You've vanquished the foe and bowed him to your will."

"You don't look very vanquished."

His eyes twinkled. "I put up a good front."

A soft knock sounded on the door. "And there's your bellboy to lead you to your well-earned rest. Sleep well, Damita."

She gazed at him in bemusement for an instant before she started to turn away.

"Oh, by the way, you wouldn't care to tell me

about those two hundred and fifty men before you go? Where the devil were you?"

She glanced over her shoulder. "Peru. I'm a construction engineer. I was building a bridge across a gorge in the Andes."

"A construction engineer," he repeated. "That may pose a few problems."

Her brow wrinkled in puzzlement. "What do you mean?"

"Nothing." He jammed his hands in the pockets of his robe. "Run along. I'll call you this afternoon."

"After you call Myra?" she asked tartly. Then she could have bitten her tongue. What difference did it make to her what woman he called?

"Myra?" His tone was vague. "Oh, we'll have to see. Good night, Damita."

Cam stood gazing after her when the door had long been closed behind her.

Damita Shaughnessy. A faint smile touched his lips as he savored the textures of the name, a combination of the earthy and the exotic. It fit the woman well. Not that she realized that she was exotic. Damita seemed to think she was both prosaic and dull compared to Lola, a view he would have to correct in the near future. She would have to be made to understand that a woman's true beauty was mostly inward and Damita's inner colors shimmered just as brilliantly as Lola's surface attraction.

But he had bought the time to do it and he would make every moment count. He had learned a long time ago to seize opportunities as they presented themselves, and he wasn't about to let this one pass—not when that opportunity happened to be Damita Shaughnessy.

The smile was still on his lips as he turned back to the phone and pressed the number of the switchboard. "Connect me with the overseas operator."

Damita gazed wearily at the suitcases that the bellboy had just delivered.

She should unpack and then shower but was too tired to do either, she decided. Tomorrow would be soon enough. She quickly stripped off the filmy blue robes and slipped naked into bed, pulling the covers up around her shoulders. She nestled her cheek in the smooth coolness of the pillow and found she was suddenly wide awake.

Her meeting with Cameron Bandor had been most unsettling, and she was still tense, her senses wired with the same heady exhilaration she had felt in his presence. It was probably a common reaction to Cameron Bandor, she told herself. He was an unusual man with a multitude of ever-changing facets to his personality. It was natural for her to be aware of the sexual magnetism of the man.

Aware? She smiled ruefully in the shadowy dimness of the room. Oh, yes, there was no question she was aware of Cameron Bandor. His physical presence as well as the fascinating complexity of his personality had shaken her to the core and aroused her to a pitch she had never believed possible.

Not that a fascination so shallow would last, she assured herself quickly. It was pure sexual attraction and probably had a stronger effect because she'd never been similarly drawn to any other man. This time next week she would be with Lola, and she would have forgotten both Cameron Bandor and her odd reaction to him.

Now she would dismiss him from her mind and think of what was important to her. Damita firmly closed her eyes and forced herself to relax. Yes, she would forget Cameron Bandor and think only of Lola.

Two

"Awake, sleeping beauty. There's a journey to be made."

Damita drowsily opened her eyes, fighting her way up through the mists of sleep. Blue eyes. Laughing blue eyes in a face that was almost sinfully handsome. Cameron, she thought vaguely. Strangely, she felt no discomfort at seeing him in her bedroom, only a sense of something wrong that had come right.

"Hello," she whispered.

"Hello yourself." The laughter faded from Cameron's face, and it became intent. "It's time for you to come with me, luv. Are you ready?"

Of course she was ready, she thought dreamily. She had been waiting all her life for him to say those words. "Why didn't you come before? There were times when I needed you so . . ."

"Were there?" His fingertips gently stroked the hair at her temples. "Well, I'm here now and I'll try to make up for all those years when I wasn't."

His touch felt as soothing to her as Lola's when she had been ill as a child. No matter where in the world Lola was, she always came to Damita when she was sick and— Her body stiffened as shock jarred her fully awake. "What—" She jerked upright, the sheet falling to her waist. She shook her head to clear it of the last clinging tendrils of sleep. "What are you doing here?"

Cameron's lips twisted with regret. "I think you knew a minute ago. Too bad." His gaze fell on her naked breasts and his voice suddenly thickened. "Lord, you have beautiful breasts. Full and round as—" She snatched up the sheet and held it to her chin, and Cameron shook his head ruefully. "Damn, I always did have a big mouth. That should teach me a lesson if nothing else does."

Bright flags of color touched her cheeks. "You should have knocked. You may own the hotel, but there's such a thing as courtesy."

"I did knock. You didn't answer, so I let myself in with the master key." He dropped down into the cushioned chair by the bed, his gaze still on the sheet veiling her breasts. "Do you always sleep this soundly?"

"Yes." She clutched the sheet closer and then realized the movement only served to reveal what she'd tried to conceal. "I have to set two alarm clocks every night." She drew an exasperated breath. "What difference does it make?"

"It makes a lot of difference. I intend to make an in-depth study of your sleeping habits." He smiled. "Very in-depth, Damita."

"Mr. Bandor, I know you think it's funny to—"

"Cam," he corrected her. "And I don't find anything about our relationship amusing. I've never been more serious in my life."

"Then why are you smiling?"

"Because I'm happy," he said simply. "It makes me happy to see you in my bed."

"This isn't your bed." She frowned. "Well, perhaps in the technical sense, but it's not really." She scowled as she saw that he was laughing. "You know what I mean."

He nodded. "Yes, luv." He straightened in the chair. "Now, as much as I'm enjoying looking at you in my technical bed, I think we'd better be on our way, sleeping beauty."

"You called me that before. I'm not sleeping and I'm certainly no beauty."

"Oh, but I still believe the name applies. I was thinking last night that you were a little like Aurora, hidden in her castle by a thousand prickly bramble bushes." His smile faded and his expression became grave. "Only you're the one who plants the bushes to protect yourself and keep everyone else out."

"Nonsense." She glanced away. "You don't know anything about the way I think or feel."

"Don't I?" His lips curved in a curious smile. "We'll see. Now, will you please get up and get dressed? I want to be at Kasmara before dark."

"Kasmara?" Sudden hope lit her face as her gaze swung back to him. "You're taking me to Lola?"

"Well, it's the first step," he said evasively as he stood up. "I've ordered the helicopter to be waiting on the landing pad on the roof of the hotel in thirty minutes. That should give you time to shower and get dressed." His glance went to the two suitcases by the door. "It's a good thing you haven't unpacked yet. I'll send for a bellboy to take your bags up to the landing pad." He turned and headed for the door. "I have to make a phone call to Damon to let him know we're coming but I'll meet you on the roof in—"

"Wait one minute," she interrupted crisply. "What do you mean, the first step? I'm not going anywhere unless I know that Lola is at my final destination."

"She will be." Cam smiled warmly. "Don't worry, Damita, kidnapping is more Damon's style than mine. I believe in trying civilized methods first."

"Damon?"

"Damon El Karim, my cousin. He'll be our host for the next few days. You'll like Kasmara. All women do. It's like something from an Arabian Nights dream."

"Like this hotel?" she asked dryly.

He shook his head as he opened the door. "Nope, this is as phony as Disneyland. Kasmara is the real thing."

"And Lola is there?" Damita persisted.

He shook his head. "But like I said, it's the first step."

"I'm not going," she said flatly.

Cam's easy smile disappeared. "You'll go. You have no choice. I'm in charge and it's Kasmara or nothing." His eyes were suddenly glacial. "Do we understand each other? No Kasmara, no Lola."

She glared at him. "I understand that you're a ruthless, self-serving son of a bitch."

"Such language." He shook his head reprovingly. "I'm sure you didn't learn that in the convent. I think I'm going to have to keep you away from those construction sites in the future. You're obviously picking up bad habits."

"Bad habits! You're the one who—"

"Easy." He held up his hand to stop the sputtering flow. "I was joking. If that's the career you want, I'm sure we can come to some compromise."

"Compromise? What the devil do you mean?"

"You give a little, I give a little. Isn't that what compromise usually means?"

"Yes, but you're—" She stopped and ran her fingers through her hair, causing the short waves to stand up in wild wisps. "I don't know what the hell you're talking about."

"You will," he said calmly. "The roof. Thirty minutes."

The door closed behind him.

Damita sat gazing at the door for a moment, torn between bewilderment and anger. Cameron Bandor was without a doubt one of the most complex men she'd ever met. Just when she was certain he was nothing but a flippant playboy, he changed, deepened into something much stronger, perhaps even dangerous.

He had said he was in charge, but she couldn't let him control her. Men would never control her life as they had controlled Lola's. She would fight against any attempt with everything in her.

She drew a deep breath and tried to organize her thoughts. She had to find Lola, and Bandor was her only lead. Why not let him think he was controlling the situation if it made him happy? He had promised to take her to Lola eventually, and she had an idea that the maddening man would keep his word.

She threw the sheet aside, jumped out of bed, grabbed her suitcase, and laid it on the bed. She rifled through it until she found underthings, jeans, and a white cotton knit sweater. Then she moved quickly toward the bathroom.

Where the devil was this Kasmara, anyway?

Kasmara lay a few hundred miles north of Marasef in an oasis in the Sedikhan desert, and from the air it looked as exotic as the Taj Mahal. Cool-looking aquamarine pools and lush, elaborately landscaped gardens surrounded an enormous palace that was stunning.

"Your cousin isn't by any chance some kind of caliph?" Damita asked dryly as the helicopter began its descent to the landing pad. "You didn't mention he lived in a palace."

"Not a caliph, but you're close. Damon is sheikh of the El Zabor and he doesn't occupy the palace most of the time. He inherited it from his mother, who was a Tamrovian but he prefers to live with the El Zabor for most of the year. He returns to Kasmara only to conduct business and indulge his more western whims."

"El Zabor?"

"The El Zabor are bedouins," Cam said. "The tribes wander the desert as their ancestors did hundreds of years ago and their customs have changed very little. I think that's why Damon has to get away occasionally. The sheikh is treated with almost superstitious worship by the El Zabor. I imagine being monarch of all you survey can put a hell of a lot of pressure on any man."

"Surely no one has that kind of power in this day and age?"

Cam smiled. "You haven't been in Sedikhan very long or you wouldn't say that. Did I forget to mention that Damon is also a second cousin to Alex Ben Rachid?"

"The ruler of Sedikhan?" Damita asked. "Does that mean you're related to him too?"

"Distantly, on my mother's side. My mother was married twice. She was half Sedikhanese and half Swiss, and her first marriage was arranged by her parents to a Sedikhanese industrialist who was forty years older than she."

"But that's terrible," Damita said, shocked. "Like something out of the dark ages."

He shrugged. "It was the custom. I was born three years later, but I never really knew my father. He died when I was two. When I was ten she married an Australian who owned a sheep station in the outback."

"Was that marriage her choice?"

"Oh, yes." Cam's lips twisted. "She was her own mistress with a huge fortune by that time. She married Bandor because she loved him. Unfortunately, Bandor loved his sheep station and her money more than he did my mother, and it didn't take her long to discover it."

"She divorced him?"

"No. She believed in keeping her promises no matter what the consequences. She stayed with Bandor until he died and then returned to Sedikhan."

"She should have divorced him," Damita said fiercely. "He used her."

"Yes," he said quietly. "But she had made a promise."

She gazed at him, incredulous. "You don't mean you think she ought to have stayed with him even though she knew he had married her for her money?"

"I'm saying it was her choice." He met her gaze. "And I believe in promises too. We need to believe in something in this cynical old world. If we can't believe in each other, we have nothing. When a promise is given, it must be kept."

"Without exception?"

"Without exception," Cam said flatly. "Of course, I'm speaking only for myself. I'd be pretty stupid to condemn someone else for not living by my code." He suddenly smiled. "What's wrong? You look as if I've grown two heads."

"It's not the kind of philosophy I'd attribute to an international playboy. It's rather . . . stern."

"Yes, it is," he said calmly. "And that's why I'm careful about the kind of promises I make. There's no way out for me." He added softly, "Absolutely none." He was holding her gaze with mesmerizing intentness, and she felt suddenly breathless. She tore her glance away and smiled with an effort. "That's good. Then I can count on you to keep your promise about taking me to Lola."

The helicopter landed gently on the tarmac and she caught sight of a tall man dressed in western clothes hurrying toward them from the direction of the palace, followed closely by a young woman garbed in flowing white robes. "Is that your cousin?"

Cam reluctantly shifted his gaze from her face. "That's Damon." He opened the heavy door of the helicopter and jumped down on the tarmac. "Come on. I'll introduce you. I think you'll find him interesting."

Damita wasn't sure he would prove interesting, but the man was certainly dashing, she thought as she stepped from the helicopter. Damon El Karim was very simply dressed in khaki trousers and a cream-colored shirt and should have looked casual and unassuming. He did not. He wore the clothes with such royal panache and moved with such feline coordination that he effortlessly caught and held the attention. She found herself looking for resemblances between Cameron and his cousin but found very few. The sheikh's complexion was darker than Cameron's, sun bronzed to a shade nearer copper than gold. His hair was also darker and worn rather long. His features weren't as classically perfect as Cameron's, his cheekbones were too broad, his lips too sensual, his green eyes too . . . too what? She hesitated, trying to put her finger on it. Then it came to her. Too passionate. The man coming toward them was charged with strong emotion that was revealed in everything about him. The leashed energy of his movements, his restless glance, the aura of power he exuded. She unconsciously braced herself as he stopped before them.

His gaze rested on her face as he took her hand. "Welcome to my home, Miss Shaughnessy." His eyes were cool as he studied her. Then suddenly he smiled. "What big eyes you have. Has Cam been maligning me again? I don't really devour little girls like you for breakfast."

"No, he hasn't . . . I mean he . . ." She found she was stammering and forced herself to take a deep breath and start over. "How do you do, Sheikh El Karim. Thank you for your invitation."

"Damon." The sheikh's eyes were twinkling. "And

I didn't expect you to be this polite. From what Cam told me on the phone, you're not exactly a willing guest here at Kasmara."

"That's not your fault," Damita said with a baleful glance at Cameron. "I'm sure this delay is entirely his idea."

"Entirely," Cam murmured, shaking hands with El Karim. "I claim full responsibility for my iniquitous conduct."

"It *is* iniquitous," she said fiercely. "You have no right to keep Lola's whereabouts a secret from me. Is she near here?"

"Not exactly," Cam said.

"Not exactly?" Damita took a step closer, her dark eyes blazing. "Then why the devil am I here? You said—"

"I'm sure you'd like to see your quarters," Damon said quickly. He snapped his fingers, and the white-robed woman rushed toward him. "Liande will show you to your suite and serve you while you're here. If there's anything you need—"

"Just snap my fingers?" Damita said testily. "I don't think I could bring myself to do that to a human being. It's like whistling for a dog."

Damon chuckled. "I assure you my servants don't take the same offense you do. It's the custom."

"It's denigrating," Damita said.

"Then you may summon them in any way you choose." Damon bowed. "As you may summon me, your humble servant, Miss Shaughnessy."

She smiled reluctantly at the thought of this

blatantly arrogant man running to do anyone's bidding, much less her own. "Fat chance." She turned toward the young servant girl who was looking at her in wide-eyed surprise. "My name is Damita and I'm very glad to meet you. Will you please take me to—"

"Certainly," Liande interrupted nervously with a sidewise glance at Damon. "Whatever the master wishes, whatever you wish." She turned and fled like a frightened white bird across the courtyard toward the palace.

"Master." Damita repeated the word as if it left a sour taste in her mouth. "I can't believe it."

"Believe it," Cam said. "I told you the El Zabor were behind the times."

"Centuries behind the times," Damita muttered as she started across the courtyard. "Incredible."

The sheikh and Cameron watched until Damita disappeared into the palace before Damon said thoughtfully, "She says exactly what she thinks, doesn't she? I believe I like her."

"So do I." Cam signaled the helicopter pilot to take off before turning back to Damon. "And more."

Damon's brow lifted. "Is that a warning?"

"Yes."

"I believe I'm hurt," Damon said mockingly. "When have I ever tried to steal a woman from you, Cam?"

"Never," Cam said bluntly. "But I know you, Damon. You're accustomed to using sex to wind down, and you're charged to the limit right now. Just don't try using Damita."

Damon's eyes narrowed intently on Cam's face. "Even if the lady is willing?"

"It would be a mistake."

Damon studied him for a moment. "I think you're right," he said slowly. "I would not risk losing your friendship to bed any woman. It wouldn't be worth it to me." He smiled. "But I think she may be worth it to you."

"She'll be worth it." Cam smiled back at him. "If I can fight my way through all the bristles and thorns to get to her. She's as wary of me as a little porcupine. It's not going to be easy."

"But you're too used to easy." Damon began to stroll across the courtyard. "This will be a nice change for you. I take it you won't want the services of a *kadin* this visit?"

Cam shook his head.

"I didn't think so." Damon smiled. "Commitment?"

Cam's gaze went to the keyhole arch through which Damita had disappeared. "Commitment," he said quietly.

"Do you like this suite? The furniture was specially made in Morocco and the carving on the doors is much admired." Liande moved forward, threw open the elaborate white doors, and gestured to the purple-shadowed hills in the distance. "I hope you enjoy the view. If not, I will—"

"The view is beautiful," Damita cut in. "The

entire suite is fabulous. I'm sure I'll be very happy here."

An expression of relief banished the anxious frown from the servant girl's face. "That is good." She moved across the room to the huge bed draped in turquoise-colored silk. "The bed is very comfortable, but I could have the mattress changed if it is not to your liking. I know Mr. Bandor would not mind. He always tries to please his *kadins*."

Damita stiffened. "Why should it matter to Mr. Bandor if I don't like my mattress?"

Liande smiled reassuringly. "But I told you it would not matter. He is most indulgent with his—"

"*Kadins*," Damita said grimly. "What on earth is a *kadin*?"

Liande's smile faded. "You're angry? I've displeased you? Forgive me, *lallah*. Shall I send you a servant who is more worthy?"

For heaven's sake, the girl would burst into tears in another minute, Damita thought with exasperation. She deliberately suppressed her impatience and said gently, "I'm not displeased with you. I think you're very . . . worthy."

Liande smiled tremulously. "Then you will not tell the sheikh I have offended you? I am very happy here. I would not wish to be sent back to my tribe in disgrace."

"You might be better off," Damita muttered. Then, as the girl's expression showed alarm, she said quickly, "And you haven't offended me. I'm sure we'll become great friends."

Liande's eyes widened in surprise. "Oh, no. I would not presume. I know you are far above me. Perhaps someday I will be thought worthy of becoming a *kadin* such as you but—"

"What the devil is a *kadin*?" Damita interrupted.

"Why . . ." Liande's expression was bewildered. "Oh, you do not understand the word. I forgot you were a foreigner. *Kadin* is a word for your most honorable profession."

"A *kadin* is an engineer?"

"Engineer?" Liande shook her head. "No, I mean . . ." She gestured to the bed. "You are the giver of great pleasure. You know the ways to bestow delight."

Damita's lips tightened. "A *kadin* is a whore?"

"Oh, no," Liande said, aghast. "I would never call you such."

"And you assume I'm Mr. Bandor's whore?"

"*Kadin*," Liande said frantically, her eyes filling with tears. "*Kadin*. I would never—"

"It's all right, Liande," Cam said from the doorway. "I'll explain it to the *lallah*."

"She is angry with me," the servant girl said brokenly. "I am stupid and unworthy."

"I am *not* angry with you," Damita said between her teeth.

"I will be sent back to my tribe. The sheikh will—"

"I'll explain it to the sheikh. It's just a misunderstanding. I think you probably managed to hit Miss Shaughnessy on an extremely sore spot,"

Cam said as he moved toward Damita. "Now, why don't you draw a bath for the *lallah*? I'm sure she'd like that."

"She would?" Liande cast Damita an uncertain glance.

She'd gladly swim the English Channel to stop the girl from weeping, Damita thought desperately. "I'd love a bath," Damita said. "Please, Liande."

"Oh, no please. It would be my pleasure." Liande hurried toward the arched doorway on the far side of the room. "Perhaps you would like a massage too? I'm very good at massage."

"That would be lovely," Damita said resignedly.

"Five minutes and all will be ready." Liande disappeared through the arched doorway.

"What's wrong with that poor girl?" Damita asked. "I've never seen such a doormat."

"Different customs. I told you this was the real thing."

"Where servant girls aspire to be prostitutes?" Damita asked caustically.

"A *kadin* isn't a prostitute. She's a woman trained to give pleasure in much the same way the geisha is in Japan. It's an honorable profession here in Sedikhan." He smiled. "Of course, there's special emphasis put on training in the sexual arts."

"An emphasis that I'm sure you and your cousin encourage."

"As a matter of fact, Damon doesn't encourage

the practice. He's forced to accept it, but he's been trying for years to bring the people under his dominion out of the past and into the present. It's not an easy task. It's considered a great honor for Damon to accept a woman from any of the tribes into his household and an even greater honor if he takes her into his bed. That's why Liande was so horrified at the thought of displeasing you. She'd be an outcast if she were sent back to her tribe."

"Barbaric."

"Perhaps, but she's far better off here. Damon has all the women of his household tutored by—"

"Tutored in what?" Damita asked.

"My, how suspicious we are." Cam's eyes twinkled. "Not in the sexual arts. Liande will be prepared to enter the university at Marasef. Why should he bother to train little innocents like Liande, when his chieftains fight to send him *kadins* who will please him?"

"And he uses them?"

"Both the chieftains and the *kadins* would be insulted if he didn't. As I said, it's a different culture."

"And one that convinces women that to be a whore is something glorious instead of degrading," she said bitterly. "How very convenient for the males of the El Zabor."

"Yes, very convenient," Cam admitted. "But then, most primitive societies are slanted to favor men."

"Not only the primitive."

Cam's gaze searched her face. "You're really upset about this. I told you that Damon was trying to make changes. It takes time to alter traditions that have been held for centuries. It can't be done overnight."

"I know that, but it's not fair." She was silent a moment, and then burst out, "I hate the idea of women being used. I *hate* it."

"I know you do." He took a step closer, his gaze intent as it held her own. "It will never happen to you, Damita."

"You're damn right it won't," she said fiercely. "I won't let it."

He shook his head. "No," he said softly. "*I* won't let it. I'll see that no hurt comes to you ever again."

It was a moment before she could tear her gaze away from his. "You have no responsibility for me," she said breathlessly.

"Then why do I feel responsible?" He reached out and brushed a wisp of auburn hair back from her temple. "I think that from now on I'll always feel responsible for you."

"Are you making a pass at me?" she asked bluntly. "If you are, it won't do you any good. I told you, I don't share my mother's lovers."

"No, my prickly little cactus flower, I'm not making a pass." He smiled ruefully. "And did I ever say I was Lola's lover?"

Her eyes widened. "No, but everyone knew you were. The newspapers . . . Of course, you and Lola were lovers."

"I hate to destroy your image of me, but I don't go to bed with every woman I meet."

She felt a rush of emotion that bewildered her. "You didn't go to bed with her? Why not?"

"The subject never came up. It wasn't that kind of relationship."

She moistened her lips with her tongue. "What kind of relationship was it?"

"We're friends," he said simply. "We liked each other the moment we met. She's a fine, intelligent woman."

"And that's all?"

"That's all." His tone was empathetic. "Thank heaven that's all. We're going to have enough problems without worrying about a complication like that."

"Complication?"

He nodded. "You've been waltzing around me like a mongoose around a cobra." He touched her cheek with his index finger. "Lord, you have wonderful skin. It feels like warm satin."

Her flesh felt as if it were burning beneath his light touch and her heart began to slam against the wall of her chest. "Does it?" He was so close that the heat from his body seemed to surround her and the clean scent of soap and aftershave drifted to her in an intoxicatingly sensual cloud. Her breasts were swelling, pushing against the material of her bra. What was happening to her? It was like nothing she had ever felt before.

"After you left last night I lay in bed and thought

about touching you." Cam's fingers moved slowly down her neck. "I wanted to reach out and touch you so much when you were sitting in the chair gazing at me. I wanted to open that skimpy little jacket and free your breasts." His fingers moved to the hollow of her throat, and he smiled as he felt the sudden leap of her pulse. "I wanted to hold them in my hands and squeeze and play with them. I'd like to do that now. Will you let me, Damita?"

She could almost feel his hands on her body, the gentle pressure of the palms. A jolt of tingling heat was spreading through her body, centering between her thighs. It was suddenly hard to breathe. She took a deep breath to force air into her lungs, but it did little good. Her breasts lifted and fell with every shallow breath and seemed to ripen and become heavier with each passing second. "I don't . . ." She trailed off, held helpless with fascination. "Cam . . ."

"You'll like it," he whispered. "I'll be so gentle with you. So loving."

Loving. What a beautiful word, she thought dreamily, and Cam's face was beautiful too. His deep blue eyes were shining with eagerness, and his smile was tender, almost sweet. She unconsciously moved a step nearer.

"Yes?" he asked. "Shall I tell Liande to leave us alone?"

She wanted him, she realized with amazement. She wanted him to touch her, to move his body against her own. She wanted to feel his muscular hardness against her softness. The desire rising within her was so intense that it was close to pain. Uncontrollable, insatiable hunger.

Uncontrollable. The thought sent panic rocketing through her. She would *not* lose control. She would not let herself become mindless with emotion. "No!" She took a hurried step back away from him and experienced a sudden poignant loneliness. "I don't want you to touch me."

Disappointment clouded his face. "Yes, you do.You want me to touch you as much as I want to do it. It's those brambles getting in the way again."

"You're talking nonsense. Perhaps I do feel some sort of chemical attraction toward you, but that's no reason to jump into bed. I'm not Myra what's-her-name or one of those *kadins*. I have to feel more than a casual—"

"You're the one who's talking nonsense," he said roughly. "There's nothing casual about the attraction between us. It's damn well explosive, and you know it. And I'm aware of exactly who you are. You're Damita Shaughnessy." Some of the anger faded from his expression and his voice softened. "My Damita."

She shook her head. "No, I don't belong to anyone but myself."

"Mine," he repeated flatly. "I knew it the moment you took off that idiotic veil last night. It was a hell of a shock to me. I never thought love at first sight existed. Sex, maybe, but not love."

She gazed at him in bewilderment. "Why are you saying these things? This has to be some kind of line."

"I'm saying them because they're true. What can I do to convince you?" He hesitated and then asked slowly, "Will you marry me?"

She gazed at him, stunned. "You're crazy. We've just met. We don't know anything about each other. You can't mean it."

"I mean it. I was going to wait for a while before declaring my intentions, but you're such a wary little bird, I thought I'd better get it out in the open. Otherwise you'd spend the next few days suspecting me of dastardly motives."

"Dastardly? You sound like a Regency rake." She was trembling, she realized. "This is some kind of joke, right?"

"Call my bluff," he said quietly. "I'll have a priest flown in tonight. I'm sure Damon can cut through the red tape."

"It's ridiculous." She tried to laugh. "You're impossible. I didn't come here to get married."

"How do you know?" He smiled faintly. "Maybe it's kismet."

She tried to hold on to some semblance of reason. "Lola. I came to find Lola."

"Soon. Should I send for the priest?"

"Of course not."

He made a face. "I didn't think you'd do it. As I said, you're a very suspicious lady." He started to turn away. "Well, if you change your mind, I'm at your disposal."

"Cam . . ."

He glanced back over his shoulder.

"You *were* joking?"

He shook his head. "No way."

"But why?"

"I told you why."

"But I can't believe you."

"I know you can't." He smiled with beguiling sweetness. "I guess I'll just have to convince you. That will be the fun part. Since my intentions are clear, you won't mind if I try to seduce you, will you, love?"

She felt the color warm her cheeks. Blast it, she seemed to be doing nothing but blushing since the moment she met him. "You can try, but it won't do you any good. That's not why I'm here."

"But you'll need something to while away the time." Cam's eyes glinted with mischief. "And I promise to make this occupation very gratifying for you." He opened the door. "Dinner is at eight. Liande will show you the way to the dining room."

The door closed softly behind him.

Three

"I've decided that you must tell me where Lola is right now," Damita said belligerently the moment she entered the dining room. "If you won't take me to her I have at least a right to know—"

"Good evening, Damita." Cam was sitting at a long, gleaming table and rose politely to his feet. "You're looking gorgeous. I like you in pink. It's an unusual color for redheads, isn't it?"

"I hate generalities. There's no reason why redheads can't wear some light shades of pink." She frowned. "Are you trying to distract me? After you left this afternoon I thought for a long time and came to a few conclusions."

"All of them wrong probably," Cam murmured. He gestured to the seat across the table from him. "But sit down and tell me about it. Damon said he'd be a little late for dinner. Some minor squabble among two of his chieftains."

She sat down and immediately attacked Cam. "It's foolish for you to not be open with me."

Cam sat down again and looked across at her. "I think I've been more than open with you." He gestured to one of the hovering servants to pour wine into her glass. "Try this. It's a Sedikhanese vintage grown by one of Damon's neighbors, Philip El Kabar."

"I don't want any wine." She leaned forward. "Why won't you listen to me? Can't you see it would be better for both of us if you'd just tell me where I can find Lola so that I can leave? This situation is becoming entirely too complicated."

"You've grown a whole new field of brambles, haven't you?" Cam looked down at the wine in his glass. "And I guess you've completely discounted my declaration of eternal devotion?"

"Yes," she answered flatly. "Though I do believe you may think it amusing to go to bed with me because I'm different from the women you usually have your affairs with."

"You're certainly different," he agreed. "But making love to you isn't my idea of an amusing pastime." He lifted his gaze to meet hers. "I have an idea it will tear us both to pieces."

She felt the hot color stain her cheeks and hurriedly took a sip of wine. "All the more reason to avoid it. I have no desire to lose my equilibrium in any relationship. You may feel free to indulge in whims, but I have a career to think about."

"And I don't?" His tone held a sharp edge. "I work damn hard, Damita. You may think of me as a playboy and you may not be far off the mark. I've always believed in stopping to smell the roses before they fade. But that doesn't mean my work isn't important to me."

"I didn't say you were a playboy."

"But you thought it."

"What else was I to think when the newspapers—"

"*Damn* the newspapers!" His eyes were suddenly blazing. "You're just growing more brambles to shut me out. Whatever I did in the past doesn't concern us. We started a new page when you walked into my bedroom last night."

"You can't wipe out the experiences that make us what we are."

"No, but we can use those experiences to pave new roads to understanding instead of letting them inhibit and close us in."

"I'm *not* inhibited."

He smiled derisively. "Hell, I can feel you withdraw into a tight little ball every time I get within two feet of you. You want me as much as I want you, but you won't drop that armor."

"I just don't happen to think this is the time or place to start a romantic interlude."

He leaned back in his chair, his eyes narrowed on her face. "Excuses."

Her hand tightened on the stem of her glass. "I don't have to excuse myself to you or to anyone."

"But you do admit I appeal to you sexually."

"No, I won't—" She stopped. She was lying both to him and to herself, and that wasn't like her. She had always prided herself on her honesty. "Yes."

"Then let me come back to your suite after dinner."

"No."

"Why not?" he asked softly.

"I told you: that's not why I am here."

"But you're such a liberated, independent woman of the world." His tone was mocking. "If you can take care of yourself in the Andes with two hundred and fifty men, surely you can handle one harmless jet-setter like me under far more civilized conditions."

"Of course I could. I just don't happen to want to."

"I'm devastated. And here I was told I was irresistible. All right, I'll up the ante. You want to know where Lola is, right?"

"You know I do."

"Then I'll make a bargain with you. You give me an hour in your bed and I'll tell you where she is." He smiled coaxingly. "One hour, Damita. That isn't asking so much, is it? I'll even promise not to do anything you don't want me to do. You can stop me anytime you like. You'd be in full control."

An hour with Cam on that silk-covered bed in the suite upstairs. Heat was spreading through her body at the thought, and she had to swallow to ease the sudden tightness of her throat. "You said you'd tell me anyway."

"But not immediately, and you're a very impatient lady. Before I leave your suite tonight, you could have the information you want. Aren't you tempted?"

She was tempted. Excitement was curling through her, making her almost light-headed. She could at last know where Lola was. All she had to do was to let Cam touch her, let him do all the things her body wanted him to do. She suddenly stiffened. "I'm not a whore. I won't sell myself."

Cam's eyes twinkled. "I'm the one who's selling. You can limit me to pressing a chaste kiss on your dainty little pinky if you choose." He sobered. "It's just a bargain, Damita. I wouldn't take anything you didn't want to give." His voice deepened to velvet softness. "You're my love."

"I know that isn't true. You couldn't—"

"I do," Cam interrupted. "A bargain?"

She hesitated. She suddenly knew she *wanted* that hour even though it filled her with an odd sense of panic. "I'd be in control?"

"All the way."

She took a deep breath and then let it out shakily. "Very well. One hour."

His smile flashed warmly. "You won't regret it."

"I'm already regretting it." She moistened her lips with her tongue. "I'm not sure this is a very smart move."

"I'm sure," he said softly. "We need this, Damita."

She could see the pulse in his temple suddenly escalate its tempo as his gaze wandered from her face, down her throat to linger on her breasts. "But I sure as hell don't need this dinner drawn out for very long. I'm not going to be able to taste anything. I'll be remembering how pretty your breasts are and how your nipples turned hard and rosy when I looked at them. I'll be thinking how I'd like to—"

"Stop." Her voice sounded strangled even to her own ears. "Not now."

"Why not? I like the idea of your knowing that every time I look at you tonight I'll be thinking of you lying on the bed with nothing on." A dark flush was mounting to his cheeks and his lips looked heavy, sensual. "And I'll be there with you. I'll be able to touch you, run my fingers down to—"

"Am I interrupting something?" Damon El Karim stood in the doorway, an amused smile on his lips. "I believe I am, but that's all right. After dealing with those idiots for two solid hours I refuse to withdraw tactfully. I feel the need of conversation with civilized human beings for a change." He moved forward to the chair at the head of the table, and a servant was instantly at his elbow pouring his wine. He lifted the glass to his lips. "They're like quarreling children. Lord, I am tired of it."

Cam reluctantly shifted his gaze to Damon. "For the moment. Next week you'll be telling me how far they've come in the past year. You know you love them."

"They're my people, my family." Damon added dryly, "That doesn't mean I don't want to break their stubborn necks when they start this kind of foolishness."

"What was the quarrel about?" Damita asked.

"A woman." Damon lifted his glass in a half-mocking toast. "The root of most discord."

"I thought that was money," Damita snapped. "Do you always interfere in personal quarrels?"

"It's one of my duties. I have the final judgment." Damon shrugged. "I had to decide which man should have the woman as wife."

"And she'll abide by your decision?" Damita asked, incredulous.

"She has nothing to say about it," Damon said wearily. "She slept with a man other than her betrothed and he's still besotted by her. Unfortunately, the other man wants her too. She must marry one of the two men or her parents will be disgraced. They'll cast her from their tent and she'll either have to become a camp prostitute or leave the tribe."

"But that's not fair," Damita said. "Can't you stop it?"

"I'm trying, dammit," Damon said harshly. "Do you think I enjoy acting like some kind of god? I hate it. But only someone wielding absolute power can make even the snall inroads I've managed so far. Two years ago there would have been no question of the girl's fate. It wouldn't have been a choice as to which man was to have her. She

would have been left alone in the desert to die
when the tribe moved on."

"But that's unthinkable. Savage."

"We're a savage people." Damon tossed down
the rest of his wine in one swallow. "And we may
stay that way if I can't manage to pound some
sense into the thick heads of those damned
chieftains."

Cam burst into laughter.

Damon gave him a scowl and then smiled sheep-
ishly. "As you very well know, I'm a savage too,
but I am trying to become civilized."

Cam's eyes were twinkling. "When you're not
pounding heads."

"I stand corrected. When I'm not pounding
heads." Damon set his glass down on the table,
and a servant was there instantly to fill it. "But
I'm tired of thinking about the entire mess. Tell
me what's happening in Marasef."

"The usual." Cam launched into an account of
a party he had attended at the palace the previous
week.

Damita sat back in her chair, her gaze fixed
thoughtfully on the two men. There was obviously
a close bond between them, and yet their person-
alities were really nothing alike. Cam possessed
none of the savagery to which the sheikh admitted. Cam was civilized, witty, charming, casting
out a glow of warmth that was nearly tangible. Yet
there was something similar about them that she
couldn't quite identify. Then Cam's gaze shifted

again to her face and her breath stopped. Sensuality. That was the common denominator. Cam and Damon were both tough, masculine, and infinitely sensual.

"I'd like to introduce you to him sometime," Cam said. "I think you'd like him."

Who? she wondered desperately. She hadn't heard a word he had said in the past few minutes. Oh, yes, he had been talking about a party at the palace.

"Your mother thinks he's one of the finest artists who ever lived. She bought a Rubinoff when she was here."

Lance Rubinoff, she thought with relief. "So she wrote in her last letter. I love his work."

"Perhaps I could persuade him to paint you." Cam's gaze moved over her face. "You have wonderful bones." His glance shifted to her lips. "And a delicious mouth." Then his gaze lifted to her eyes, and she felt a tingle of electricity vibrate through her at what she saw reflected there.

He wanted her. He was thinking of the two of them on the bed in her suite and what he would do to her, and he intended her to know what he was thinking. Her hand was trembling as she lifted her glass to her lips. "Why would Rubinoff want to paint me? You said I was no beauty and he has his pick of anyone."

"Did you really say that, Cam?" Damon asked. "How ungallant of you and completely out of character." He snapped his fingers. "Dinner." A stream of servants carrying silver trays that bore a selection of salads appeared as if by magic through a doorway across the room. The sheikh didn't give them a glance as he idly studied Damita. "I find you most attractive. I believe he must have been trying to intrigue you with his candor, Miss Shaughnessy. Did he succeed?"

Intrigue, charm, infuriate. Cam had managed to do all of those things to her in the short time they had known each other, and by the smile on the rascal's face he was well aware of it. She picked up her salad fork and began to eat the gelatin salad that had been placed before her. "Oh, I didn't pay any attention. Everyone in the world knows you can't take Cameron Bandor seriously."

"I shouldn't like him," Damita said with a puzzled frown. "He's chauvinistic, arrogant, and completely spoiled."

"Damon?" Cam opened the door to Damita's suite and stepped aside to let her precede him. "You're right. He's all of those things."

"But I *do* like him." Damita entered the suite and turned to face him. "Why?"

"Because he's also honest, intelligent, and capable of laughing at himself." Cam closed the door and leaned against it. "Rare qualities in a man wielding that much power. He's also more sensitive than you'd believe. For instance, I noticed Rana wasn't invited to the dinner table tonight."

"Rana?"

"His current *kadin* in residence. He thought her presence might make you uncomfortable since you were so upset about Liande's subservient attitude."

"So that poor woman has to remain alone until he deigns to notice her?"

"The 'poor' woman will be amply rewarded for her cooperation. I assure you that she's completely satisfied with her lot. It's the culture of—"

"I'm tired to death of hearing about the kind of culture that makes victims of women," Damita said impatiently. "I don't want to talk about the poor creatures anymore."

"Neither do I." Cam smiled faintly. "Though I'm glad the subject aroused your interest enough to present a distraction tonight. I was afraid you'd have second thoughts, but I think you completely forgot our little bargain."

Damita could feel the color warm her cheeks. She hadn't forgotten but had feverishly grasped at the opportunity to submerge the memory. She had been excruciatingly aware of Cam all through dinner and had welcomed the distraction the sheikh offered. "I didn't forget." She turned away jerkily. "What . . . How do we go about this?"

Cam straightened away from the door. "First, you relax. You act as if I'm going to chain you to the bed and beat you."

"I feel . . . awkward." She didn't look at him. "I don't think this is going to work. Let's forget about it."

"Oh, no." His voice held a thread of tension. "We definitely won't forget it. Physically it's impossible to do so now."

"Is it?" Her gaze flew down his body and the color deepened in her cheeks. Arousal. Stark and bold. She moistened her lips. "I'm sorry but—"

"Hush," Cam said softly. He moved toward the arched doorway leading to the bathroom. "Undress while I run you a hot bath. That should help you relax. I'll call when it's ready."

Damita breathed a sigh of relief as he disappeared through the archway. She doubted if anything could relax her. She was so tense, she felt as if she'd shatter if Cam so much as touched her. Yet it was a strange tension that caused the muscles of her stomach to clench and a throbbing to fill the emptiness between her thighs.

"Undress." It was Cam's voice from the bathroom. How had he known she hadn't moved, she wondered. Then she heard the sound of water running into the sunken tub she had used before dinner. She could back out, she thought. Cam was no barbarian. He would never force her.

But she didn't want to back out, she realized suddenly. The bargain they had struck had only been a flimsy excuse she had seized upon to take what she wanted. Cameron Bandor had drawn her like a magnet since the first moment she had seen him and was drawing her now with irresistible force.

She moved slowly toward the bed, where Liande

had laid out her white cotton nightgown and tailored navy blue robe. She hesitated, staring down at the garments. Then, not giving herself a chance to think, she quickly kicked off her high heels and began to take off her clothes.

"Damita."

She reached hurriedly for the navy blue robe and slipped it on. The silky nylon felt cool against her warm bare flesh. She needed that coolness. She felt as if she had a fever. "I'm coming."

She walked quickly to the arched doorway, trying not to think what lay on the other side.

He was naked.

She had seen Cameron naked last night, but this was different. His nudity had seemed almost casual then, but there was nothing casual about him now. He was all sexually aroused male.

"Don't look at me like that. I'm not going to eat you." Cam's eyes gleamed. "Well, not now anyway. I make no promises for later. You're much too appetizing." He motioned to the enormous white marble tub that was filled with frothy bubbles. "Your bath awaits. Unlike Damon, I have no hang-ups about my male dignity. I'll even act as maid-servant."

"That won't be necessary. I can—" She broke off as Cam took a step forward and started untying the belt at her waist. The heat emanating from his body enveloped her as he pushed back the edges of her robe. Then he was looking at her, his gaze running over every curve with intimacy and possession. She felt her nipples harden as if he were touching them.

"Beautiful. What a gorgeous body you have, luv."

She shook her head. "I'm okay. But I'm a little too plump." Her voice sounded breathless. "And I'm much too short."

"You're just right." His gaze moved up to meet hers. "For me."

Something hot and infinitely pleasant rippled through her, and she found herself smiling happily at him. "You're easily pleased."

"You'll find me so, but I've been known to be damned picky where other women were concerned." He pushed the robe from her shoulders and it fell in a pool on the marble floor behind her. "But that's in the past. I won't have to worry about that now, will I? Neither of us will." He frowned in sudden concern. "But do I please you?"

How could he not please her? He was tough and lean and magnificently male. "You're very . . . nice." She turned and quickly started down the steps of the tub. "Not that it matters. Our bargain was for one hour, not a lifetime." She sat down in the tub and found to her relief that the bubbles covered her to her shoulders. "And ten minutes of that time has gone by already."

"Then I'd better make the most of the moments I have left." Cam sat down on the edge of the tub and then slipped into the tub facing her. "Lean back and relax."

She inhaled sharply as his palm touched her belly beneath the water.

"Relax," he repeated, rubbing gently. "Do you like this?"

"I don't . . . know." Pleasure and pain conflicted. "I think so."

His fingers moved down. "And this?"

She swallowed. "Yes."

His fingers probed carefully. "Lord, you're tight," he murmured. "Ease up, sweetheart, I don't want to hurt you."

She bit her lower lip. "I can't—" She gasped. Another finger had joined the first, and heat streaked through her. "Cam, it's too—"

"Did I hurt you?"

She tried to steady her breathing. "No."

"But I will if you don't relax." He frowned in concern. "You're back is stiff as a board. Why are you so nervous with me? I won't hurt you."

"I don't know," she whispered. She felt the tears rise to her eyes. "I don't *know*."

"Shh. It's all right." Cam pulled her into his arms, enfolding her and rocking her tenderly. "You'll be fine in a minute. I guess it's too soon for you."

It didn't feel too soon, she thought miserably. Even now the wiry brown hair on Cam's chest was pressing against her breasts, and she could feel a hot shiver run through her with every breath she took. His arms were so strong around her and the sheer maleness of him was drawing her with primitive power. She wanted desperately to reach out to him, touch him, but her muscles seemed locked.

His fingers were in her hair, fluffing, tangling in a caress that was more affectionate than passionate. "Easy, luv. You're so sweet. Can you feel how much I want you? Your hair is soft as a duck's feathers. I like these little wisps and curls." His voice went on, praising her, gentling her, wooing her.

It went on for a long time. "Damita?" Cam's voice was inquiring.

She didn't know how to answer him. No one had ever been this tender with her. She wanted desperately to give him what he wanted from her, but she couldn't seem to do anything but take from him.

He suddenly released her and stood up, reaching down to lift her to her feet. "Come on."

"Where?" she asked, startled.

"Out of here." He lifted her to the side of the tub and levered himself up beside her. "It's not working, you're not . . ." He trailed off as he reached for a towel and dried himself sketchily. "I can't figure out what's wrong," he muttered. "You *want* me. I know damn well you want me. Did I hurry you too much? What the hell is the matter?"

"I told you I felt awkward. I'm not . . . You're angry. Let's just forget it."

"No way." He reached for another towel and knelt beside her. "And I'm not angry. I'm frustrated as the devil, but I'm not angry with you."

Relief poured through her. "You're not?"

He began drying her shoulders. "Why should I

be? You're not fighting me." The rough terry grazed her nipples, and he smiled grimly as he saw the instant response. "At least your body's not. You do want me, Damita?"

"Yes."

He finished drying her and threw the towel aside. His gaze fastened on her breasts and his head bent slowly. "I love your breasts. They're as ripe and plump as perfect melons." His mouth closed over her nipple and he sucked gently.

Her heart began to slam against her rib cage. Fire. Hunger. Her nails dug deep into her palms.

"Touch me," he whispered. "I want to feel your hands on me. I want that so much."

She *wanted* to touch him. Her body was on fire. Starved. Why couldn't she move? It was as if she were locked in a cage and unable to free herself.

His palms were cupping her breasts, squeezing and releasing as his mouth and teeth nibbled and pulled at her taut nipple. "Give to me, Damita."

She made a sound low in her throat that was strangely like an animal in pain.

His gaze flew to her face and he froze as he read the torment there. "You can't," he said in wonder. "My God, you *can't* respond." He closed his eyes for a moment and drew a deep shaky breath. "Hell and damnation."

"I don't—" She stopped. She didn't know what to say. "I'm sorry."

His eyes flicked open. "You're not the only one." His movements were jerky as he stood up and began to dress. "Why the hell didn't you tell me? Is it just me or the whole male sex?"

"I didn't know," she said numbly as she reached for her robe. "It never came up before."

"It never came up?" He glanced over his shoulder. "What do you mean, it never came up."

"I've never . . ." She tied the belt of her robe and glared at him. "I'm a virgin, dammit."

"A virgin," he repeated, stunned. He turned to face her. "For heaven's sake, you're twenty-three years old."

"So what?" she asked defiantly. "I've never wanted to do it before, and now I know why. I'm probably frigid or something."

"You're not frigid. You're as responsive as TNT. There's just something holding you back and I wish to hell I knew what it was."

So did she, Damita thought wearily. Her body was still throbbing, aching with a hunger that had not been satisfied. She tried to smile. "I'm sorry I was such a dud. I know you expect a better performance from your partners. Better luck next time. Maybe you could call the sheikh and get him to send you a *kadin*. You said they don't mind and I wouldn't really blame you if—"

"Shut up!" he said roughly. "I'm not going to call anyone. This is between the two of us and we'll work it out together."

"There's nothing to work out." Her smile was brittle. "It was just an experiment that fizzled. Now we're right back where we were before. Would you mind leaving? I'm very tired and I'd like to be alone. I know I promised you an hour but perhaps—"

"You know that bargain was just an excuse." He shook his head. "Though heaven knows why you need an excuse. It's *right* between us, Damita."

"Evidently you're mistaken." She crossed her arms to try to suppress the sudden chill she was feeling. "It certainly wasn't right a few minutes ago."

"Something's wrong, dammit." He took an impulsive step toward her and then stopped. "I want to hold you but I can't. Not right now." His face was taut with strain. "I'm still horny as the devil and I don't think either of us could cope at the moment."

"I certainly proved that I couldn't," she whispered. "Please leave, Cam."

"I will." He stood looking at her, desire and frustration conflicting in his face. "Lord, I don't want to go. As soon as that door closes behind me you'll begin building new walls to shut me out."

"You're already shut out. It shouldn't have happened."

"That's a bunch of bull." His blue eyes flashed with sudden anger. "It should have happened and it *will* happen. Make up your mind to it."

She shook her head. "Are you going to tell me where Lola is? I know I cheated you and didn't fulfill my part of the bargain."

"Will you be quiet?" Cam's voice was hoarse. "I can't take much more. You didn't cheat me. I'd rather have had the little you gave me than an entire night with one of Damon's *kadins*. You're not a failure. I'll find a way to—" He drew a deep breath. "Look, I've got to get out of here. I'll try to think about this and see what I can come up with as a solution, but right now I can't think at all. I can only feel." He turned and started for the arched doorway. "I'll see you tomorrow morning." He paused and turned around to face her. "Lola is at Half Moon Bay."

"Is that near here?"

"No." His lips twisted in a mirthless smile. "It's a hell of a long way from here. It's a Bandor property outside Sydney, Australia."

He turned on his heel and went through the archway. A moment later she heard the door of her suite close behind him.

Four

"Good morning, Miss Shaughnessy." Damon's gaze raked Damita's face as she entered the breakfast room. "Or am I being too optimistic? You look as haggard as Cam this morning. Sit down and have breakfast with me. Perhaps some vitamin C will help." He snapped his fingers. "Orange juice."

A servant sprang forward to seat Damita and then pour orange juice into the crystal goblet beside her plate.

Damita flinched. "I wish you wouldn't snap your fingers."

"Sorry, I forgot you didn't like it." Damon smiled. "It's difficult to break the habits of a lifetime. That's how things are done among the El Zabor."

"So Cam told me." Damita made a face. "Custom."

"Exactly." He started to snap his fingers and

then stopped and turned to the hovering servant. "Breakfast for Miss Shaughnessy."

The servant stood there, uncertain.

"Breakfast," the sheikh repeated.

The man gave him a bewildered glance and then hurried from the room.

Damon shook his head ruefully as he turned back to Damita. "It's much quicker my way."

"But not as courteous." Damita found herself smiling at him. "Since you're trying to civilize the El Zabor, perhaps you should start closer to home."

"Ah, but that's always the hardest battle to be fought." Damon's green eyes gleamed with humor. "It's much easier to get rid of the barbarity in others than in myself."

Damita lowered her eyes as she spread a napkin on her lap. "You said you've seen Cam this morning? Where is he?"

"He went riding with me at dawn but said he had some calls to make and would have breakfast later." He lifted his coffee cup to his lips and gazed at her over the rim. "He was very quiet this morning. Did you refuse him your bed?"

Her eyes widened. "That's none of your business."

"He's my cousin and my friend. That makes his happiness very much my business." Damon's voice had a sudden steely edge. "I want him to have what he wants. I'd be happy to give you any little trinket you fancy to make sure that will come to pass."

"You're incredible. I'm supposed to jump into bed with Cam just to make *you* happy?"

"I'm sure it would make Cam even happier than it would me. He's quite taken with you."

"He's quite taken with the entire female sex."

He shook his head. "It's true he enjoys women, but I think what he feels for you is different."

"In what way?"

He leaned back in his chair and gazed at her thoughtfully. "I'd say it was the difference between a playful breeze and a cyclone."

Damita felt a swift surge of emotion that she tried to hide with a careless shrug. "My, what a melodramatic comparison. How can you tell the difference? You don't impress me as a man who regards women as possessing any great amount of power."

"Oh, I believe they possess power." His lips twisted. "No one knows that better than I do. I've just found one must channel that power in the proper direction if one is to survive."

There was some other emotion beneath the mocking cynicism in his voice, Damita realized. Pain? Whatever it was, it vanished in the next instant as he smiled at her. "So what's your decision? Will you let me give you a little incentive to speed things along in the way both you and Cam obviously want them to go?"

She should have been furious with him and she would have been if a moment before she hadn't been enlightened by that look of vulnerability in him. "What would you give me?" she asked curiously.

"What would you like? I'm really abominably rich. A car? Perhaps a piece of jewelry from Tiffany? Whatever you choose."

"And all to give Cam what he wants," she said slowly. "You must care for him a great deal."

"He was kind to me when I needed kindness." He took another sip of coffee. "We went to the same boarding school in Paris when we were boys and I didn't take to the idiotic rules and regulations."

A tiny smile tugged at her lips. "I can see how you'd have problems."

"Because I'm an arrogant bastard?" He nodded. "Without Cam I would have exploded and taken the whole damn school with me. But everyone liked Cam and he managed to run interference for me for six long years. It wasn't easy for him. He took a hell of a lot of flak."

"I see." She could imagine Cam in the role of a mediator, trying with infinite patience to keep Damon on an even keel in an environment so foreign to him. But Cam had been alone and away from home too. Who had been there to comfort him, to form his bedrock of security? "Cam's obviously missed his vocation. If he was able to keep you under control, he should have gone into the diplomatic service."

Damon read the softening in her face and pounced. "You do like him. Why not give him what he wants? I'll have my secretary make arrangements with—"

"No." She held up her hand. "I think you've been associating too long with *kadins*. I don't take bribes."

He was silent a moment. "Most women do, you know. If not in one form, then in another." He studied her before saying slowly, "But I think you mean it."

"I do." The servant set a plate of luscious-looking melon before her. "Now, can we talk about something else?"

"You won't change your mind?"

"No."

He sighed. "Then I suppose I'll have to leave it up to Cam. He can be very persistent, but sometimes his methods are a tad too civilized to my way of thinking."

"He said you were more likely to use kidnapping as a means to an end than he was."

He chuckled. "He knows me very well. But few women are worth the trouble that would result from kidnapping."

The man was truly impossible, she thought resignedly. "I take it you believe in playful breezes instead of cyclonic relationships for yourself?"

He nodded. "No cyclones for me." He smiled. "Though I have no objections to a sirocco now and then."

"A sirocco?"

"It's a strong, hot wind that blows over the desert. It touches, takes your breath away, and then it's gone. No devastation. Just—"

"Will you excuse us, Damon?" Cam stood in the doorway. "I have to talk to Damita."

"She hasn't finished breakfast," Damon protested. "And I'm sure she's been so fascinated and charmed by my conversation that she has no desire to desert me for a boring fellow like you."

Damita set her fork down and jumped to her feet. "I'm finished." Her heart was pounding and she felt a trembling start in the pit of her stomach as she looked at Cam. Damon was right, Cam did look strained and his expression was more grave than she had ever seen it. "I've been waiting to talk to you about Lola."

"I thought you would be." Cam gestured. "Let's go to the library."

Damon shook his head. "You do realize my ego is dragging in the dust? Oh, well, what can you expect when a cyclone hits."

Cam frowned. "Cyclone?"

"Never mind." Damon snapped his fingers and a servant hurriedly refilled his cup with coffee. The sheikh smiled at Damita. "You see how I fall back into bad habits when deserted by civilized influences? Are you sure you wouldn't rather stay and save me from myself?"

"She's sure," Cam said curtly. "Stop playing, Damon. I'm not in the mood."

"I can see that." Damon waved them out of the room with a grandiose gesture. "It's clear that neither of you can furnish me with either entertainment or a role model in your present state. You may leave."

"Thank you," Cam said dryly. "We intend to do just that." He took Damita's arm and turned her toward the door. "Will you call Marasef and have them send the helicopter?"

"You're leaving Kasmara?" Damon's smile faded. "How soon?"

"I'd like to arrive in Marasef by late afternoon."

A shadow of disappointment flickered over Damon's face and then was gone. "I'll arrange it. It will be as easy as . . ." He glanced at Damita, his eyes suddenly sparkling like those of a naughty little boy up to mischief. He deliberately held up his right hand and snapped his fingers. "That."

The servant behind him stepped forward and then stared at the sheikh in confusion as Damon motioned him away.

Damita shook her head, trying to suppress a smile. Incorrigible. Simply incorrigible.

"Come on." Cam impatiently propelled her from the room and down the hall. His tone sharpened. "You and Damon seem to be getting along famously. Perhaps you'd like to stay here a few more days."

"I think he's lonely," Damita said slowly. "He is disappointed that you're leaving. He really cares about you, Cam."

The annoyance faded from Cam's face. "I know he's lonely. He lets very few people get close to him. I wish—" He stopped and shrugged. "I can't try to solve Damon's problems right now. We have enough of our own. Aren't you going to ask me where we're going?"

"Would you tell me?" she asked dryly. "I'm becoming accustomed to being whisked from place to place willy-nilly. I assume this time you're actually taking me to Lola?"

"Yes." He opened the door and stepped aside for her to precede him into a richly furnished book-lined room. "I was tempted to keep you here for a little longer. Lord knows, we need time alone to straighten out this mess. But I knew you'd probably try to cross the Sedikhan desert barefoot rather than stay here now that you know where Lola is."

"Yes, I would." She drew a shaky breath. "And we really have nothing to straighten out."

"The hell we don't. Did you sleep last night?"

She didn't answer.

"Well, neither did I." He lifted her chin on the arc of his finger so that he could look into her eyes. "And I have no intention of leaving things at the status quo so that I'll be in danger of having more nights like that one."

A sudden river of joy ran through her, taking her off guard. She hadn't realized until this minute how afraid she'd been that Cam would have had second thoughts after her withdrawal. But he still wanted her.

"Don't look at me like that," he said thickly. "I'm having enough trouble keeping my hands off you. I'm trying to prove how restrained and considerate I can be."

She suddenly felt terribly vulnerable and shy. "You were very kind to me last night," she said haltingly. "I'm sorry I disap—"

His fingers on her lips silenced her. "For heaven's sake, did you expect me to force you? I *care* about you, dammit."

The joy came again. Stronger this time, so strong it frightened her. She took a quick step back. "Why did you bring me here to Kasmara when Lola is in Australia?"

"I needed the time. I figured a few days one way or the other wouldn't matter to Lola but they mattered a hell of a lot to me."

"Then Lola isn't really out of touch?"

"Not completely. She's staying at a small line shack about five miles from Half Moon. There's no telephone there, but it took only a couple of hours for the foreman to drive over, verify your story and drive back."

"And she's all right?"

"She's fine," he said gently. "She says she's enjoying herself out in the wilds."

"Lola?" Damita shook her head in disbelief. "That's hard to believe."

"You can ask her yourself day after tomorrow. I have the Bandor company plane waiting at the Marasef airport to take us to Sydney. We'll stay the night at the hotel there and drive out to Half Moon the next day."

"Why not go to Half Moon immediately?"

He hesitated. "It may not be safe. I want to make sure there's no way we can be followed."

"Safe?" Damita echoed with sudden panic. "Who would follow us? You said Lola was fine."

"She is," he said soothingly. "And we want to make sure she stays that way."

"Why shouldn't she be safe?" Her eyes blazed up at him. "What's this all about, dammit?"

"I was beginning to think the bramble bushes had begun to dry up and disappear." He shook his head. "Not yet, right?"

"You can't say something like that and expect me to take it calmly."

"No, I guess not. I'd probably feel the same way."

"Then tell me what's happening."

He shook his head. "I don't think I have the right. I'll let Lola tell you."

"Cam, for Pete's sake, I'm her daughter. I have a right to know if she's in trouble. Why—" She stopped in exasperation as she saw the resolute expression on his face. "You're a very stubborn man."

"I made Lola a promise that I'd keep her alive and well," he said simply. "In my book, that also means not breaking her confidence."

In spite of her frustration she experienced a sudden flood of warmth toward him. No, Cam would never break his word. Not to Lola and not to her. Promises were important to him. The realization gave her a feeling of security greater than any she had ever known. "Very well." She whirled on her heel and started for the door. "Have it your own way."

"No arguments?"

"I don't have time. I've got suitcases to pack."

She opened the door and made a face at him over her shoulder. "Again. This had better be the last time, Cam. I'm getting tired of being bounced around the world."

A smile lit his face with warmth. "The last time. I promise, luv."

Promises again. She wanted to stay and look at him. "I'll hold you to that particular promise," she said lightly. The next moment she was gone.

Cam stood there for a long time after she had left. She was changing toward him, her guard easing, her sharpness losing some of its sting. The alteration was definitely noticeable and filled him with a hope so heady it made him almost dizzy. It was only a start, but maybe if he was patient . . .

The problem was that he didn't feel at all patient. For the first time in his life he wanted to react as wildly and violently to restraint as Damon or his brother, Jordan, did.

But he couldn't lose patience now. For to lose patience might also mean losing Damita.

The lobby of the Sydney Bandor was colorful, spacious, and its luxurious furnishings had a distinctly Australian flavor. The pièce de résistance was a glass atrium in the center of the lobby complete with eucalyptus trees and several live koalas.

"I don't believe it," Damita said, shaking her head in amusement. "And I thought the Marasef hotel was bad. What do you have in the Beijing Bandor? A panda bear?"

Cam shook his head. "We considered it, but they're an endangered species and need very special care. We settled for creating walls with aquariums complete with exotic fish and a giant statue of a red dragon in the lobby."

"And I suppose all the maids wear cheongsams?"

"Certainly. What else?" Cam pushed the button for the private elevator. "It's expected."

"Why?" Damita gazed at him curiously. "Why all this phony atmosphere? You said yourself that it was strictly Disneyland."

"Sure it is." The doors of the elevator slid silently open and Cam waited until they had entered the elevator to continue. "But Disneyland is fun. Why not provide a little make-believe when good service goes with it? People need to get away from their problems occasionally and just float away into never-never land." He shot her a sidewise glance as he pushed the button for the penthouse. "I bet you've never been to Disneyland."

"Why do you think that?" Damita asked defensively.

"Have you?"

"Well, actually I haven't been there." She rushed on. "But not everyone likes to indulge in make-believe. I had my career to think about and I had plenty of good times without going to amusement parks."

"And it was far too frivolous a pastime for a girl

with her feet firmly planted on the ground," Cam said quietly. "Pretty illusions aren't at all practical and can be dispensed with. Right?"

"You make me sound like a stick-in-the-mud." Damita frowned. "I did have to work hard, Cam."

The door slid open and he grasped her arm. "I don't doubt it. You had to prove to yourself and to everybody else that you weren't a sex object like your mother." His hand tightened on her arm as he felt her stiffen, and he urged her out into the lushly carpeted hall. "I wonder if that's why you chose engineering as a profession. It put you on a level with men and had nothing to do with—"

She jerked her arm away and whirled to face him. "I became an engineer because I have a passion for building. Why do you think you know everything about me. I *like* what I'm doing. Is that clear? And if I wanted analysis, I'd go to a psychiatrist."

Cam's eyes twinkled. "Why should you go to strangers when I'm at your disposal?" He unlocked the door of the suite. "And I don't pretend to know everything about you, but I can make a damn good guess when I draw a blank." He drew her into the apartment and closed the door. "I've done a hell of a lot of thinking these last few days about what makes you tick."

"Should I be flattered?" she asked tightly. "You make me feel like some kind of a freak."

"I don't mean to." His tone was weary. "I'm just looking for something to grab on to to keep me from grabbing on to you. It wasn't easy keeping my hands off you on the plane trip here."

She felt a rush of relief. "It wasn't? I thought—" She stopped. "You've been very remote since we left Kasmara. I thought you'd changed your mind." She continued quickly. "Not that it matters. I wouldn't have blamed you if—"

He was kissing her—hard, hot, taking her breath as well as her words. When he lifted his head they were both trembling.

"I don't change my mind," he said hoarsely. "And it does matter. It matters to me and I hope to heaven it matters to you too. Does it?"

She lowered her eyes. "We've just met. I don't know . . ."

He shook her. "Don't hem and haw, dammit. I need to know you feel something for me besides a hormone surge. I have to know if this hell I'm going through is worth it."

She slowly lifted her gaze to meet his. "You're . . ." She swallowed and tried again. "I do care for you."

Some of the tension ebbed from him. "A little anemic but it's something anyway. How much?"

Her eyes filled with tears. "I don't know. I think about you all the time. I feel warm when you smile at me. I want to know what you're thinking and what you're feeling. Is that enough?"

"No, I want a hell of a lot more than that." He smiled with an effort. "But it will have to do for now. Maybe the flashing comets and supernova's will come later." He released her and took a step back. "At least it's a start."

Damita stared at him uncertainly.

"I know I'm rushing things," he said gently. "We'll take it one step at a time from now on." He gestured to the door to the left of the sitting room. "That's your room. I have to phone Damon. I picked up a message from the desk that he'd called and wanted me to call him back. After that I'll order dinner in the suite for eight. Why don't you try to nap for a few hours?"

"I'm not tired." She was suddenly reluctant to leave him. She wanted to stay near him, watch the expressions on his face, listen to the inflections of his voice. It was oddly like an addiction, an emotional dependency. Panic shot through her. She didn't want to be dependent on any man. Not ever. She quickly turned away and opened the door. "But maybe I'll rest for a while. I'll see you later, then."

The door closed hurriedly behind her, as though she'd taken flight, Cam thought.

Cam shook his head ruefully as he turned and strode toward the phone on the end table by the long white leather couch. Damita was taking one step forward and a half step back, but he supposed that was better than standing still. He picked up the receiver and requested the overseas operator. Three minutes later he was connected with Damon at Kasmara.

Damon issued no salutation. "Are you all right?" he asked tersely.

"Why shouldn't I be all right?" Cam asked. "It was a smooth flight and the customs men were very understanding about the pouch of diamonds I was hiding under my shirt."

"Very funny." Damon's tone was not amused. "I'll tell Rosol how lighthearted you are about all this when I visit him in the hospital."

Cam instantly sobered. "Who's Rosol?"

"One of the kitchen servants here at the palace. He drove to the village for fresh vegetables and was picked up by two gentlemen who asked a good many questions about you, Damita, and any other guests who might have visited me in the last two months."

"Damn! Then I was being watched by Belstrop's men after all. There wasn't a sign of them at the hotel in Marasef for the last two months."

"It would seem they're very good at their jobs. They were quite rude to Rosol when he refused to give them information about you."

"How rude?"

"Two broken ribs, a bruised kidney, and internal bleeding."

"Damn them to hell," Cam said bitterly. "Lord, I'm sorry I involved you in this, Damon. What can I do to help Rosol?"

"Nothing. He's mine and I'm caring for him." Damon added grimly, "And those particular men won't bother you anymore. I had them picked up and sent to the chieftain of Rosol's tribe for judgment with word that I was very displeased with them."

"You're sure they're Belstrop's goons?"

"Oh, yes, they spoke quite freely when they found that the El Zabor could be even more rude than they if circumstance demands it. They had orders to find Lola and thought you might lead them to her. They weren't sure what connection Damita had to Lola but said Belstrop was making inquiries."

Cam was chilled by the news. Belstrop was known as relentless. It probably wouldn't take him long to find out that Damita was Lola's daughter no matter how carefully Lola had hidden it. And when Belstrop found out, he would realize Damita was a weapon he could use. Hell, he might know already. "Then this hotel is probably being watched. Any report would turn up the fact that I spend a good deal of time here."

"And it's reasonable to assume Half Moon will be under surveillance too," Damon said. "That's why I called to warn you. Otherwise I would have waited until I got there to—"

"You're coming here?" Cam asked. "Stay where you are, blast it. I've involved you enough. I won't let you risk anything more."

"Let?" Damon enunciated the word as if it were totally foreign to him. "Belstrop's men injured one of mine. *Mine.* Do you think I'll permit that to go unpunished?"

Cam knew very well that Damon would do nothing of the sort. The part of him that was pure El Zabor was in blazing ascendancy. "No, I guess not. Come ahead, but don't expect me to wait around so that you can stick your head in the communal noose."

Damon chuckled. "I'll find my own noose. But if you run across Belstrop, save him for me. I want him." Damon hung up.

Cam swore softly under his breath as he replaced the receiver. All he needed was to have Damon arrive at Half Moon on the vengeance trail. It was going to be ticklish enough trying to keep Damita safe and remove Lola from Half Moon before Belstrop found out where she was. It was a foregone conclusion he'd have to find another hiding place for Lola.

He needed *time*, dammit. He knew Damita was drawing closer to him but he had wanted to give her as much slack as possible in the silken ties that would bind them. She had to grow accustomed to him.

Belstrop's appearance on the scene had blown that possibility to smithereens. He might even have to isolate Damita with her mother until it was safe for both of them to surface. He would probably not have any time at all with Damita before events would intercede to take her from him.

He had only tonight.

Five

Blast it, why hadn't she brought something feminine to wear besides the pink dress, Damita wondered despondently as she gazed in the mirror. There were distinct disadvantages in traveling light. She supposed the boat-necked sheath was attractive enough, but Cam had already seen it and she wanted to . . .

She wanted to do what? Seduce the man, for heaven's sake? Any attempt to do that would probably result in the same debacle as had occurred in the room in Kasmara. She had acted like the original ice maiden, and there was no guarantee she wouldn't freeze up again. If she had a shred of good sense, she would shy away from anything approaching intimacy with Cameron Bandor.

A soft knock sounded at the door and her heart

gave a sudden leap, and she promptly forgot the advice she had just given herself. "I'll be right there." She turned away from the mirror, hurried across the room, and threw open the door. Cam was there, wearing a white dinner jacket that contrasted stunningly with his dark brown hair and tanned skin. Damita found herself gazing at him like a lovesick teenager. "Hello," she said breathlessly.

"You're wearing that dress I like so much." Cam smiled with the genuine pleasure of someone who'd just been given a present, and Damita felt as if Cinderella's rags had turned into a ball gown. He switched off the overhead light before taking her hand to draw her into the sitting room. "I thought we'd dine on the terrace. There's a great view of Sydney Harbor from here."

"Fine." Her voice was a little husky, and she quickly cleared it. "Did you get in touch with Damon?"

"Uh-huh." He opened the sliding door and stepped onto the lushly landscaped terrace, leading her toward a candlelit table by the stone balustrade. "He may decide to join us at Half Moon."

"Why would—" She broke off and inhaled sharply as she gazed out over the city. The view of the harbor wasn't only beautiful, it was magical. The lights ringing the shore formed a glittering diamanté necklace against the velvet of the night, and the waters of the harbor were silvered with starlight. "I don't think I've ever seen anything so lovely."

"That avant-garde butterfly structure across the way is the opera house," Cam said. "They're doing *Otello* this evening. Would you like to go? But perhaps you don't like opera. It seems to be an esoteric taste in this day and age."

"I've been only once. *Madame Butterfly*." She made a face. "The music was beautiful but I thought she was pretty stupid."

He chuckled. "Her feet were definitely not planted firmly on the ground. I gather you'd never be so swept away?"

"Right." She sat down in the chair he was holding out for her. Her tone sounded reassuringly firm in spite of the fluttering in her stomach. She had the uneasy feeling that just being in Cam's presence was sweeping her away, making her lose the moorings she had clung to for a lifetime. "Do you like opera?"

"I like it, but it's a little slow for me." He sat down opposite her and smiled at her across the table. "So we'll skip *Otello* tonight. I'm sure we can find something else to do." He took the wine from the ice bucket and poured a clear bubbling stream into her glass and then his own. "Tell me about your convent. Were the nuns kind to you?"

"Oh, yes, very kind. I had everything I could possibly want."

"Really? I would have thought your upbringing would have been on the ascetic side."

She shook her head. "The nuns were strict but wonderfully kind. Do you think Lola would have left me there if they weren't?"

"No. Perhaps ascetic was the wrong word. Were you lonely, Damita?"

"Of course not. I had the nuns, and Lola came whenever she could. And then there were the other children—" She broke off. "I guess I was lonely sometimes, but that wasn't Lola's fault. It was just the way things were." She shrugged. "It doesn't matter. Things are different now."

"You have friends?"

"Doesn't everybody?" She lowered her gaze to the clear depths of the wine in her glass. "Of course, I've been busy since I left the convent. I finished college in three years and co-oped every summer with the engineering firm I'm with now. That doesn't leave much time for keeping in touch."

"Very little time."

"It's not that I'm antisocial." She gazed at him warily. "I suppose you're going to make some sort of Freudian claptrap out of that too?"

He shook his head. "No probing tonight. I want to relax and enjoy myself."

"Then why all the questions?"

"I want to learn everything there is to know about you," he said simply. "I missed a lot of years with you and I'm trying to catch up."

She felt a melting deep within her. It was all too much—the sable beauty of the starlit night and Cam sitting across from her looking at her with a tenderness that cast its own radiance. "Can I play catch-up too?"

"What do you want to know? You'll be disappointed. I've led a fairly dull life."

"Not according to the tabloids," she said dryly.

"I told you I like smelling the roses." He smiled. "I probably lack discrimination but I enjoy nearly everything. I like practically every sport; I enjoy the theater, museums, concerts. I like most people once I get to know them. I even enjoy the hell out of my work. I'm boringly uncomplicated and— Why are you laughing?"

"Because you don't know yourself at all." Her eyes were dancing. "I've thought from the first moment I met you that you were one of the most complex men I've ever known."

He looked at her blankly. "I am?"

She nodded solemnly. "Definitely."

He smiled boyishly. "Well, I'll be damned. I was afraid you'd find me slow going after Damon. I've always been the calm port in a stormy sea to everyone else."

She gazed at him in amazement. She had thought he was so assured and self-knowing, yet he didn't realize his quiet strength and stability were every bit as magnetic as Damon's more volatile appeal. Just being with him made her feel as if she were near a glowing fire that would always be there to warm and nurture. "There's a lot to be said for tranquil ports," she said huskily.

He grimaced. "You're dead wrong. They're not talked about at all; they're just accepted."

In a way he was correct, she thought. She remembered how odd she had thought it at their first meeting when that blond bombshell had accepted her dismissal with no hint of resentment toward Cam. Now Damita understood her attitude very well. Cam was simply so loving and caring that it was impossible to believe he would intentionally hurt or insult anyone for whom he had even the most casual feeling.

"But you don't resent it, do you?"

"I'm used to it." There was the faintest flicker of wistfulness in his expression. "But I think I'd like it if you thought I was as exciting as Mikhail Baryshnikov and Harrison Ford all rolled into one. Do you think you could manage that?"

"It wouldn't surprise me." Her voice was uneven. "If you give me time to get to know you, I'm sure I can discover all kinds of interesting—" She broke off. "What's wrong?"

He forced a smile. "Nothing. It's just that there's never as much time as we'd like." The door opened and a serving cart was wheeled onto the terrace by a white-jacketed waiter. "Dinner." Cam shifted his shoulders as if throwing off a burden. "I ordered a few Australian specialties."

"If you tell me we're having koala stew, I'll never forgive you."

"I'd never forgive myself; it would be like eating Smokey the Bear. Does lamb offend your sensibilities?"

The lamb was delicious and followed by dishes of comparable excellence—not that Damita paid close attention to what she was eating. She was too busy listening to Cam's droll stories and watching the expressions on his face. As the evening progressed, she began to feel as light as air, as if she could float over the balustrade at any minute. She couldn't remember ever feeling this young and full of joy or laughing so much over nothing at all.

Cam tilted his head as if listening to something infinitely pleasant. "Lord, that's pretty. For a while I didn't think I'd ever hear you laugh like that."

"I'm not a sad sack even if I haven't ever gotten around to going to Disneyland." Her dark eyes were glowing in the candlelight. "And I feel like laughing. I feel . . ." She made a sweeping gesture. "Oh, I don't know. As if nothing could ever go wrong again. As if this place and time could go on forever. Do you know what I mean?"

Cam nodded. *"The Secret Garden."*

"What?"

"It's a book written generations ago by Frances Hodgson Burnett. Haven't you ever read it?"

She shook her head. "I don't think so."

"It's about three troubled children who discover a deserted garden and make it their own. They heal the garden and in so doing the garden heals them. They decide it's a magic place where nothing can ever go wrong."

"A magic place," Damita said softly. "I wish there were magic places. I wish . . ." she trailed off and laughed shakily. "I don't know what's the matter with me. I'm not usually this fanciful. Maybe it's the wine."

"Or maybe you've discovered that your feet don't have to be planted in reality all the time." Cam's gaze met her own across the table. "Perhaps you're feeling it's safe to wander in magical secret gardens with someone who loves you."

Damita inhaled sharply. Cam's gaze was holding her with seductive power. She could see the rapid throb of the pulse in his temple and that his lips were no longer smiling but heavy with sensuality. She was acutely conscious of her body, the fullness of her breasts, the blood pounding through her veins.

"Damita." He reached across the table and touched her hand. It was a casual caress but her reaction to it wasn't casual. She began to tremble. The warmth of his flesh, the masculine hardness of his hand—she hadn't expected this. Suddenly warmth and safety were gone and there was only the need she had known once before. "I don't . . ." She forgot what she was going to say as his thumb began to rub the sensitive skin of her inner wrist. The muscles of her stomach clenched as waves of heat began to sweep through her body.

"It's *right*, Damita." Cam's voice was urgent. "Can't you feel it?"

She could feel nothing but heat and hunger and the power drawing her toward him. She made an effort to gather her thoughts. "It won't work. The last time—"

"Forget the last time." Cam released her wrist and rose swiftly to his feet. Then he was around the table, swiveling her chair before dropping to his knees in front of her. "You weren't ready for me. I rushed you too much." His gaze met her own as he slowly pushed up the skirt of her dress. His palm touched her inner thigh. "You're ready for me now, aren't you?"

She could feel the hard warmth of flesh through the sheer hose separating them. She bit her lip as a spasm of heat tingled through her, intensifying as it reached the center of her womanhood. She couldn't breathe and opened her lips to permit more air to her starved lungs.

He slipped off her shoes and began slowly to stroke her inner thigh. "Oh, yes, you're definitely ready for me now. I can feel your muscles tense and ripple as I touch you." He gently widened her legs, and his other hand moved up to cup her and rub with slow, skillful strokes. "Do you like that?" he asked hoarsely.

She nodded jerkily; she didn't have the breath to speak.

"Up, luv, just a little so that I can get this off you. . . ."

Then the panty hose and the bikini panties beneath them were gone, the dress pushed up even farther. Cam's gaze was like a burning touch. "You're so pretty down here." His fingertips stroked, then widened to explore. Damita bit her lip to choke back a gasp. Fire. Melting. "Like that garden we were talking about. I want to open the gate and come closer. . . ."

Cam's head was lowering and then his hard cheek was pressed against the flesh of her belly. With every word he uttered his lips feathered her with flame as his hand moved rhythmically. "You're flowering for me, aren't you? No thorns, just this beautiful giving." His teeth bit gently and a hot shiver ran through her. "Do you know how much I want you? It's like nothing I've ever felt before. I'm all tied in knots and all I can think about are the things I want to do to you here. . . ." His fingers moved, played. "And here. . . ." Another finger joined the others, and the rhythm accelerated, deepened with force and power. "And most of all, here."

She was burning up. The breeze on her cheeks had felt cool before, but now there was nothing but heat and Cam's lips, his fingers, his voice.

"I want to be inside you," he said hoarsely. "It's like a fever. I want you to hold me inside you and let me stay there forever. I want you to let me—" He stopped and lifted his head to look up at her. The skin was drawn tight across his cheekbones and his eyes were blazing. "Damita!"

He was suddenly on his feet and pulling her up from the chair, across the terrace and into the sitting room. The door slammed shut behind them. "Do you want me? If you don't, tell me now." He shrugged out of his dinner jacket and hurled it onto the couch. He pulled her into his arms, his palms cupping her bottom, and a shudder racked his body. "Hell, it may be too late already." His hands opened and closed on her buttocks as he rubbed with sensual slowness against her lower body. He closed his eyes, every muscle of his body hard, tense, aroused. "Tell me."

How could he expect her to speak when she couldn't even think, she wondered desperately. Then it was too late to do either.

Cam's eyes flicked open. "Damita, it's too— Damn!" His hands reached out, jerking the dress over her head, undressing her with fevered speed. She tried to help, but he brushed her hands aside as if she were trying to hinder him.

He pulled her down on the thick carpet, parted her thighs, and moved over her.

She gasped. "Your clothes."

"I can't *wait*." His eyes were blazing down at her and he was making adjustments to his clothing even as he spoke. His lips covered her own, his tongue playing wildly. "I have to—"

He plunged forward and his lips smothered her low cry. Then his head lifted and she could see by his expression that he hadn't heard her. His eyes reflected a blind, glazed sensual pleasure. She felt a surge of sheer primitive satisfaction that she had the power to give him pleasure so intense it made him forget everything, feel nothing but the delight she offered him.

"Tight. So tight." He began to move, carefully at first, then plunging, thrusting, stroking deeply. Filling emptiness with fullness, hunger with satisfaction. "Damita . . . wonderful."

Yes, wonderful, she thought hazily. A secret garden of beauty—delicious, hot, breathtaking, growing, blossoming more with every stroke. Her hands fluttered helplessly on his shoulders. She wanted to help, but he was moving with too much power and she could only accept.

Cam had said something about acceptance, she remembered vaguely through the veil of pleasure he was weaving about her. To accept Cam was to accept power, pleasure, and a warmth that lit the world. He would not permit her to give, so she accepted joyously, wildly, completely.

"It's like nothing—" Cam's voice was a guttural gasp in her ear. "Damita, say it's all right. Say—" He plunged deep.

Piercing pleasure, blazing radiance, hunger vanished, need fulfilled.

She heard his low cry above her, and a great shudder ran through his body.

She was panting, her lips parted to take in more air. Her lids fluttered closed as an exquisitely sweet languor possessed her limbs. This was lovely, too, she thought dreamily, to feel Cam's weight on her body and know that she had given him the same pleasure and beauty he had given her.

She was dimly aware that he was moving off her, gathering her in his arms and lifting her. She was too tired to open her eyes. "Where are we going?"

"Bed." The word was oddly clipped, and it jarred

her a little. She tried to open her eyes to look at him, but they were now in her bedroom and it was too dark to see his expression.

He placed her carefully on the bed and drew the spread over her. His movements were precise, almost mechanical, and a tiny stab of fear pierced the languor she was feeling. "Cam?"

"Go to sleep." His voice was muffled. He turned away and then stopped. When he spoke again his words were halting. "Is there anything that I can do? Did I hurt you badly?"

"No, you didn't hurt me at all."

Something was *wrong*. She raised herself on one elbow and watched his shadowy silhouette cross the room. "Are you okay?"

"Am *I* okay?" He laughed harshly. "Oh, yes, I'm just dandy." He opened the door. "Go to sleep, Damita. I'll meet you in the sitting room at nine tomorrow morning."

The door closed behind him before she could speak again.

Damita huddled beneath the silken spread, curling into a ball to ward off the chill. The warm, delightful sleepiness was gone and she was suddenly wide awake. Cam had been so brusque, almost cold to her before he had left the room. She had no previous experience to go by, but she knew damn well this wasn't the way it was supposed to be. What had gone wrong, she wondered miserably.

Perhaps she hadn't pleased him as much as she had thought. He was accustomed to experienced women and she was probably clumsy in comparison. But perhaps this was the way all men behaved after they had sex. What did she know? She shouldn't really be surprised. Hadn't she always believed that most men regarded women as something to be used and then discarded?

But not Cam.

Cam was different, kind, caring. Cam had said he loved her.

Lord, how naive that sounded. She had heard men always used the word *love* when they wanted a woman. How stupid and naive and childish she was being.

She realized suddenly that tears were running down her cheeks and impatiently rubbed her eyes against the material of the pillow. She wouldn't cry, dammit. So what if she'd made a mistake and let herself be used? No, she wouldn't lie to herself, she was no victim. She had wanted Cam to make love to her; she had wanted everything that had happened tonight. It was just that she had wanted much more. She had wanted the two of them to go on forever wandering in that lovely secret garden Cam had shown her.

But she wouldn't think about secret gardens or promises tonight. She would blank out all the raw hurt and loneliness she was feeling and go to sleep. Tomorrow she would be stronger. Tomorrow she would be able to face Cam calmly and not let him see either the hurt or the humiliation she was feeling.

Tomorrow it would be better.

Lord, what a blue-ribbon ass he had been!

Cam's hand tightened on the balustrade until the rough stone bit into his palms. The pain felt good, cleansing; he deserved a hell of a lot more punishment, he thought in self-disgust as he gazed unseeingly at the harbor lights below.

He had acted like a savage, a man without a conscience. Hell, he'd practically raped Damita, been blind to everything but his own need. Never in his entire life had he taken a woman with such mindless passion. Always before he had been able to maintain control and use gentleness to assure his partner's pleasure. But with Damita, who had needed his patience and restraint more than any woman he'd ever known, he had given neither, but dragged her down to the floor and plunged into her like a rutting animal.

He realized he was feeling a stirring in his loins even now at the thought of her warm tightness holding him. He *was* an animal where Damita was concerned, and she didn't need his barbarity. She needed understanding and gentleness, and it was no wonder she hadn't responded to his wildness. She had even seemed stunned when he had carried her to bed. Who could blame her? He had been so frantic that he'd deliberately seduced her tonight. Then to cap it off, he'd lost control and nearly raped her.

Well, this self-castigation would do no good. He would have to make reparation and try to heal the wounds he'd inflicted. He'd have to show her he could give her the restraint and patience she needed.

Restraint? He almost laughed aloud at the thought. He was as hard, aroused, and ready right now as he had been a short time before when he had pulled Damita down on the carpet and moved over her. He knew that every minute he was with her he'd remember that time and his body would respond with helpless animal instinct.

But he wasn't an animal.

He would give to her, not take. It took only strength of will. By tomorrow he would have himself under control; tomorrow the hunger would be less.

Tomorrow it would be better.

Six

"I thought you said Half Moon Bay was just out-side Sydney." Damita carefully kept her gaze on the scenery passing outside the window of the jeep. "It seems like we've been traveling for hours, and I'm sure we've been going around in circles."

"I told you I wanted to be sure we weren't being followed." Cam continued to look straight ahead. "And we aren't going to Half Moon; we're going straight to the line shack."

Damita's gaze flew to his face. "Is that safe?"

"I don't have a choice. There's a good chance Half Moon is being watched, but if we were fol-lowed from Sydney, we've lost our tail. Hold on tight."

He left the road, drove the jeep down a steep verge, and bumped along a jarring hundred yards or so before parking the vehicle behind a screen of shrubbery. "We walk from here. The line shack is about a mile beyond that hill." He jumped from the driver's seat and came around to help her from the jeep. His grasp was completely impersonal, and he released her immediately. "Stay close to me." He turned and strode quickly away through the trees.

Stay close to him? Closeness was now an alien concept in their relationship, Damita thought grimly. Cam couldn't have been more remote if he had jetted to another planet. Since he had met her in the sitting room this morning he had been a polite stranger, obviously wanting to make it clear to her that their physical encounter had been an episode that wasn't to be repeated.

Cam looked over his shoulder. "Coming?"

"Of course." She started after him, moving swiftly through the brush. She was glad Cam was being honest enough not to pretend to feel something for her that wasn't there, she told herself firmly. Her coolness had reflected his own and neither of them had mentioned the explosive passion that had erupted last night. It was over and her feeling of hurt pride—and perhaps a faint sense of betrayal—would pass. It *had* to pass, she thought with sudden desperation. She must forget about Cam and think only of Lola. "I suppose you won't tell me who you're trying to throw off the track with all these maneuvers."

"You'll know soon enough," Cam said. "The line shack is just ahead."

Damita's pace quickened as she felt a sudden surge of anticipation. Lola was close by.

"It's about time you paid me a visit, Cam. I was beginning to feel like a hermit."

The words were spoken by a woman from beyond a stand of eucalyptus trees, and the voice was wonderfully familiar. Lola's voice. Damita recognized it with a leap of eagerness.

Cam frowned. "I told you to stay in the cabin, Lola."

"Cam, my pet, I haven't obeyed any man since I was a kid in the barrios." Lola's laugh was rich and throaty, the sound of her voice closer now. "If I hadn't ignored your advice, I might be in jail." Lola thrust aside the branches of a bush and abruptly came into view. "I'll cooperate only so far with this madness. There are limits to—" she stopped as she caught sight of Damita, her eyes widening in surprise. "What the hell are you doing here?"

"Lola!" Damita ran forward and threw herself into her mother's arms. "You're really all right. I've missed you so. Why haven't you phoned or written?"

"Querida." Lola's arms tightened lovingly around Damita for a brief instant and her voice softened with tenderness. "I've missed you too. You are well?"

"I'm fine," Damita said. Everything was fine

now that she was here in Lola's arms. She caught a whiff of Lola's familiar perfume and felt a sudden sense that all truly was right with the world. Lola had used only that scent since Damita had told her how much she liked it when she was eight years old. She had a sudden desire to stay in Lola's arms, where she had always felt so secure. No matter how lonely and miserable she had felt in the past, it always had vanished when Lola held her like this. She desperately needed that sense of stability now. "Why shouldn't I be fine? You're the one who fell off the face of the earth." Damita laughed shakily. "I had to turn into a regular Sherlock Holmes to track you down."

"So I was informed." Lola's hold loosened and she stepped back, turning to Cam with a frown. "I sent word you weren't to bring her here, dammit."

He shrugged. "She was asking questions. I decided if I didn't bring her here, Belstrop might become curious as to why she was so interested in your whereabouts."

"Who's Belstrop?" Damita asked.

Lola's gaze searched Cam's face. "How much does she know?"

"Nothing," Damita said with exasperation. "He made you one of his blasted promises, remember?"

"Oh, yes, I remember." Lola's face softened as she looked at Cam. "Cam's very big on keeping promises. I guess you've found that out."

"Yes," Damita said shortly.

There must have been something in her tone

that aroused Lola's interest, for her gaze swung back to narrow speculatively on Damita's face. "It's true," she said quietly. "Take it from someone who knows."

"We'd better get back to the cabin," Cam said. "There have been a few new developments, Lola. We have to get moving."

"What's happened?" Lola took Damita's arm companionably as she started to follow Cam down the path through the brush.

"We were wrong about Belstrop not making the connection between us. He's evidently had a tail on me since you disappeared, and when Damita showed up at the hotel, his men reported it at once."

"Then why the devil did you bring her here?" Lola asked harshly. "I want her kept out of it. Why do you think I cut off all contact with her?"

"Easy," Cam said. "I didn't know about the tail until Damon called the hotel in Sydney last night. He told me Belstrop was making inquiries about Damita."

Lola's hand unconsciously tightened on Damita's arm. "Dammit, he'll find out everything."

"Who is this Belstrop?" Damita asked again. "Will someone please tell me what's going on?"

Cam glanced back over his shoulder. "Lola?"

"Colin Belstrop is an exceptionally unpleasant gentleman," Lola said grimly. "Unfortunately, I didn't realize how unpleasant until I had become involved with him. He appeared to be quite charming on the surface. He owns an art gallery in Knightsbridge and an estate in Devon. He's well connected and I thought him . . . attractive."

"He was your lover?" Damita asked bluntly.

Lola grimaced. "More like a weekend fling than a full-fledged affair. I spent four days with him at his estate in Devon." Her lips twisted wryly. "I wished to heaven I'd never gone. Colin wasn't only wretched in bed, his conversation was positively stultifying. Now, being a lousy lover is sometimes acceptable if a man has something else going for him, but don't let anyone ever tell you that master criminals are interesting. They're just—"

"Criminals," Damita interrupted. "Belstrop is a criminal?"

Lola nodded. "It turned out he's a drug kingpin who uses his gallery as a cover to import heroin and cocaine into the U.K. But of course I didn't know that until I went to Scotland Yard about the murder."

Damita shook her head in bewilderment. "You're getting ahead of me. What murder?"

"There was a murder that weekend I was in Devon," Lola said. "The very last night, which was really unfortunate. If it had happened sooner, it would have saved me a very boring weekend."

"Lola!" Damita said impatiently.

"You're always so serious, *querida*. I'm coming to it." Lola's great dark eyes were twinkling. "How did I ever have such a solemn child?"

"Murder is serious business, Lola."

"Well, I thought so too, at first. That's why I jumped into the car and drove back to London and straight to Scotland Yard. However, they informed me that Vito Mareno, the murdered man, was just as big a scumbag as Colin. He was connected with the Mafia in Rome and all sorts of other unpleasant things like murder and prostitution as well as drugs. The authorities seemed overjoyed that he was dead. Not only did they get rid of one drug king but if I testified, they could put Colin away too."

Damita held up her hand. "Wait just a minute. You saw Belstrop murder this man?"

Lola nodded. "I was standing at the bedroom window looking down into the garden when I saw Colin pull out a pistol and shoot Mareno." She pulled a face. "I bet that was the most interesting thing that's happened in that bedroom since Colin bought the estate. *Quel ennui!*"

"Lola, for heaven's sake, this is no joke. If you witnessed the murder, why is Belstrop still free?"

"Bail," Cam said. "Very expensive bail."

"Then why isn't Lola in protective custody?"

Cam's lips tightened. "Because she's a very bull-headed woman."

Lola frowned. "Those detectives at Scotland Yard would have sewn me up in a dreary hotel room for months until Belstrop came to trial. They were very polite and charming, but I wasn't about to let them do that to me."

"So she made a statement and flew back to

Marasef," Cam said. "She actually intended to stay there at the hotel with Belstrop loose."

Lola shrugged. "Then Cam became depressingly protective and melodramatic and insisted on whisking me off to the wilds of Australia until the trial."

"Better the wilds of Australia than the morgue," Cam said grimly. "You knew Belstrop would be after you."

"Why else am I here?" Lola smiled at him, her face suddenly radiant with warmth. "I very much like living, thank you. Particularly when I have friends like you worrying about me."

The frown faded from Cam's face. "I'd worry less if you'd worry more. You're taking Belstrop too lightly."

Lola shook her head. "I never take scum lightly. I know how they can hurt you if you let them touch you. But the trick is not to let them touch you, except on the surface. You can't keep them away entirely, but you can keep them from burrowing underneath."

"Hell, not you too?" Cam's lips twisted. "Bramble bushes appear to abound in your family."

"Bramble bushes?" Lola frowned. "I don't know what you mean."

"Never mind," Cam muttered. He thrust some branches aside with barely concealed annoyance and strode ahead of them down the path. "I'll see you at the line shack."

Lola gazed after him in puzzlement. "That's not like Cam. What's wrong with him?"

Damita didn't answer.

Lola's shrewd gaze shifted to Damita's face. "Have you by any chance allowed Cam to . . ." She stopped in dismay as she saw the color flood Damita's cheeks. "Oh dear, that wasn't at all wise, *querida.*"

"I know that," Damita said jerkily. "I claim temporary insanity. It was stupid. We have nothing in common. Don't worry, we both realized it was a mistake that won't be repeated."

"I hope not." Lola's brow furrowed in a troubled frown. "You see Cam is . . . different."

"You mean he's a playboy who likes to smell the roses," Damita said dryly. "I know that, Lola."

Lola shook her head. "I mean that he's a man women not only want to go to bed with." She paused. "He's a man women love, Damita."

Damita felt a cold chill. "Do you love him, Lola?"

"Of course I love him." Lola shook her head as she saw Damita's expression. "No, not like that. There are so many ways to love. Haven't you found that out yet?"

"He said you were friends."

"We are friends. He's one of the few men I've ever met who's capable of maintaining a friendship with a woman. I think it's because he inspires so much trust."

"Does he?" Damita's glance slid away. "I don't really want to talk about Cam, Lola."

"No?" Something flickered in Lola's face and then was gone. "Then we won't discuss him." She suddenly smiled brilliantly. "Instead, you can tell me how you like my new Robinson Crusoe persona. Don't you think living in the wilderness becomes me?"

It did become her, Damita thought as she studied her mother. Lola's tall, voluptuous figure was just as attractive in the faded jeans and yellow sweatshirt as it was in her usual haute couture attire. Her dark hair was drawn away from her face in a loose bun that revealed her wonderful bone structure and accented her enormous dark eyes. She looked tanned and rested and more relaxed than Damita had ever seen her. "You look beautiful. There's an air about you, something different that I can't quite place. . . ."

"Peace?" Lola suggested.

"Maybe," Damita said slowly. "I've certainly never seen you this serene before."

"I feel serene." There was a touch of wonder in Lola's voice. "Staying here has been good for me. It's been years since I've had a chance to be alone and reassess who I am and where I want to go. I highly recommend it."

Damita looked at her in surprise. "I always thought you knew exactly who you were. You're the most together person I've ever known. I remember when you used to visit me in the convent, you'd sweep into the room and suddenly everything was bright and shining and solid again."

Lola frowned. "Was that the only time it was

like that for you? I thought you were happy at the convent. You were always such a quiet little thing that I was never sure what you were thinking."

"I was happy there," Damita said quickly. "You did everything you could to make life perfect for me. You have nothing to blame yourself for."

"I'm not so sure. I've been thinking a lot about that too, and I may have made a hell of a mistake." Lola's smile was bittersweet. "Hindsight is a marvelously frustrating thing, isn't it?"

"You didn't make a mistake," Damita said fiercely. "You gave me a good life, Lola."

"Materially perhaps."

"You were always there when I needed you."

"Was I?" Lola's gaze was fixed thoughtfully on the trees ahead. "If I'd kept you with me, it might have been better."

"You wanted to protect me."

"But instead I left you alone to learn how to protect yourself." Lola's gaze shifted to Damita's face. "That's what Cam meant by bramble bushes, isn't it?"

"Amateur psychology," Damita scoffed. "He doesn't really know anything about me."

"Cam has wonderful instincts about people. He may have seen something in you that I didn't want to let myself see."

"Nonsense." Damita smiled with an effort. "You're getting as bad as he is. Everyone can't live as glamorous and exciting a life as you, Lola. There have to be people like me to strike a balance."

"You don't think you're glamorous and exciting?"

Damita laughed. "Of course not. You're the siren of the family."

"I see," Lola said slowly. "Is that how you perceive me?"

"That's how the entire world perceives you. You're a lovely, warm, intelligent woman who just happens to be as glamorous as Helen of Troy."

"Helen of Troy seems to me to have been a very flighty female. I've always hoped I had more substance."

Lola's voice was so grave that Damita felt a flash of anxiety. "You do have substance. I didn't mean to—Oh, dear, you know how many rough edges my tongue has. I didn't hurt you?"

Lola shook her head. "No, you didn't hurt me." Her tone was abstracted. "You just gave me a little more to think about."

"Lola, will you please save the introspection until later?" Damita asked with affectionate exasperation. "Preferably until this is all over and Belstrop is no longer a threat to you."

"The case goes to trial next week. After I testify, Belstrop will be out of the picture."

"And you'll be safe."

"So the gentlemen at Scotland Yard tell me. Without a leader, Belstrop's organization will fall apart."

"Thank God," Damita said fervently. "Then we can forget about all this and go back to living our own lives."

"I'm not so sure about that." Lola's gaze searched Damita's face. "Sometimes things come along that change us and make it impossible to go back."

Pain surged through Damita, and she tried to keep her face impassive. She laughed shakily. "Are we on that again? For Pete's sake, nothing world-shaking happened between Cam and me. All I did was go to bed with an attractive man. It's not as if I were a child. I'm twenty-three years old, and most people would even consider me slightly retarded not to have had an affair by this time." Her lips twisted. "I don't doubt Cam thinks I am."

"Why do you say that?"

Damita tried to shrug carelessly. "I told you that I'm no sex goddess. I guess Cam was disappointed." Her voice was uneven, and she paused before she went on. "We're not at all suited."

"Neither were Romeo and Juliet," Lola said. "Sometimes it doesn't make any difference."

"It *does* make a difference. And we're not Romeo and Juliet." Damita tried to hold her voice steady. "Cam evidently thought of me as a challenge and I thought of him . . ." Shining promises, safety in a wild sea, tenderness and passion. "I thought of him as an experience."

"How sensible," Lola said softly. "But then, you were always sensible, *querida*. There were never any pipe dreams for you."

"No pipe dreams for me," Damita agreed. She drew a shaky breath. "Now, let's forget about me and talk about you. What have you been up to here besides all this soul searching?"

Lola was silent a moment and then obviously decided to accept the change of subject. "All sorts of primitive high jinks. You won't believe this, but I've actually learned to cook. I found this old yellowed cookbook on one of the bookshelves at the cabin and thought to myself, why not? So I started on appetizers and I've just graduated to entrees." She shot Damita a laughing glance. "And if you ask me very nicely, tonight I may honor you with my first dessert."

Seven

Lola opened the door to the small cabin with a flourish. "Here it is. My home away from home. No electricity, but there's a tiny bathroom with a shower off this room. It's a bit primitive, but you should have seen it before I got to work on it. Naturally, I had to have the men from Half Moon bring a few pieces of furniture to make the cabin more habitable. Can you believe that Cam didn't even have any cushions on the chairs? And no vases for flowers. The countryside practically exploding with wildflowers, and not one single vase."

Damita's gaze moved around the comfortable-looking room. "It's very pretty." A round rattan table and four chairs occupied the center of the room. The chairs were gaily cushioned in a yellow and cream-colored floral pattern that matched the cotton spread on the single bed against the wall across the room. The vases of wildflowers of which Lola had spoke were everywhere, on the night-stand, beside the candelabra on the table, on the bookshelf beside the door. There was even a vase on the rattan bureau to the left of an iron wood-stove that looked as if must have been built before the turn of the century.

Cam was placing a suitcase on the bed and turned as Damita and Lola came into the room. "I'm sure the stockmen who used this line shack before you never complained about the lack of cushions and vases for flowers."

"Then they should have." Lola shut the door and smiled at Cam. "You're lucky you didn't have union trouble with conditions like this. If I were going to be here much longer, I'd definitely insist on an electric generator and a ceiling fan." She tilted her head consideringly. "One of those white fans with brass trim and light fixtures that look like pretty white flowers. I'm sure it would be good for morale."

Damita chuckled. "I'll have to remember that on the next construction site I'm sent to. One of the perks has to be an elegant white ceiling fan."

"With lights like flowers," Lola reiterated firmly. "That's very important."

"You won't be here long enough to worry about ceiling fans, Lola," Cam said crisply. "I want you to start packing so that I can get you and Damita out of here right away. I called Scotland Yard late last night and the authorities in London have arranged safe accommodations for you there until you testify next week."

Lola's smile faded. "That was rather presumptuous of you. I'm going to stay here until a few days before the trial begins. I told you I didn't want to be under lock and key."

"Too bad," Cam said coolly. "Belstrop's moving in and it's going to be difficult protecting you here. You leave today, Lola."

Lola's dark eyes flashed. "The hell I do. You don't even know if Half Moon is being watched."

"I'm not going to take the chance." Cam's lips tightened. "And if you care for Damita, you won't either. Once Belstrop knows who she is, he'll try to use her to intimidate you. The only solution is to make sure you're both under police protection."

"But I don't want to—" Lola broke off as her glance fell on Damita. "Oh, very well. If it will keep Damita safe, I'll let them stash me away. But Damita and I won't travel together. I may be a target, but I won't make Damita one too."

"Damita should leave right away," Cam said curtly.

"Not with me." Lola's jaw squared and her tone hardened. "Let me lead them away from Australia and her. Then you bring her to London tomorrow."

"But I want to go with you," Damita protested.

"It's no use," Cam said. "I've run into this before. She's stubborn as the proverbial mule."

Lola made a face. "What an unflattering comparison."

"I don't feel like flattering you at the moment. I want this over and both of you safe." He paused. "Okay, I concede, Lola. You go today. We'll let Damita stay here in the cabin, as I'm sure we weren't tailed from Sydney. Then, when we know you're safe, I'll bring Damita to London. Satisfied?"

Lola nodded. "As much as I can be under the circumstances.'"

"I don't see why I can't go with you," Damita said. "You're being overcautious, Lola."

"You'll get tired of my company soon enough. We'll probably be confined in suffocatingly close quarters after we reach London, *querida*." She turned to Cam. "I suppose you've already made arrangements. How much time do I have?"

A faint smile touched his lips. "At exactly three o'clock a helicopter will touch down at Half Moon to take you to Sydney. From there the company jet will fly you to London. It will be gassed up and ready for takeoff when the helicopter arrives."

"Three? That gives me only an hour and a half. You don't drag your feet when you make a decision, do you? I'm surprised you're giving me time to pack."

"I might even let you drink one cup of coffee if you finish in time," Cam said lightly. "But only one. Then we leave for Half Moon."

"Dictator." Lola turned to Damita. "It seems I won't be able to demonstrate my new cooking skills after all. But not to worry. When we get to London I'm going to insist the authorities keep us in great style in a place with a magnificent kitchen."

Damita tried to smile. "And a ceiling fan with lights like pretty flowers?"

"Of course. Now, why don't you sit down and rest while I pack." She patted Damita on the cheek. "Don't look so serious. All will be well."

"I know it will." Damita cleared her throat of any hint of huskiness. "I'm glad you're going where you'll be safe. You should have let Scotland Yard protect you from the beginning."

"Oh, Cam's protection was much more entertaining." Lola shot him a mischievous glance. "Until now. He's being most uncharacteristically staid and practical at the moment."

"How regrettable." Cam took a large metal coffeepot from the stove and crossed the few feet to the hand pump at the sink. "But if you don't get a move on with your packing, I'm going to renege on my promise to let you have even that one cup of coffee."

"Beast." Lola turned toward the bureau. "I'll be packed in five minutes. I didn't exactly bring an Imelda Marcos wardrobe for my stay here."

Lola was packed in less than the promised five minutes and Cam and Lola were ready to leave the line shack a quarter of an hour later.

"You go ahead, Cam," Lola said briskly. "I'll

catch up to you in a minute. I want to say good-bye to Damita."

Cam paused at the door to look back at them with a frown. "You'll see each other in two days."

"Go." Lola made a shooing motion with one hand. "You can't have things all your own way, dictator. I'll be only a moment."

"Hurry." Cam closed the door behind him with a decidedly annoyed sharpness.

Lola shook her head. "I've never seen Cam this uptight. I think if I hadn't agreed to go, he would have hogtied and thrown me on that jet."

"He's worried about you."

"Is he?" Lola shook her head. "Maybe, but I'd say he's more worried about you. I found his attitude very enlightening. Particularly after observing your reaction to him. That's why I decided to stay behind for a few minutes to have a chat with you."

"Now isn't the time to have a chat," Damita said quickly. "And I told you I didn't want to talk about Cam."

"There's always time to straighten out muddled thinking, and I have an idea both you and Cam are bogged down all the way to your armpits. Believe me, it's better to get things right at the beginning. Once you get on a certain track, you have a tendency to forget about getting off." She paused. "Until you're forced to stop and think again. It took me twenty years to find out that I was on the wrong track. Don't make the same mistake I did, *querida*."

"Twenty years?"

"I'm a little slow." Lola grimaced. "I thought what I wanted was life in the fast lane. Smart parties, yachts, jet-setters as friends and lovers."

"And you found you didn't want that?"

Lola shook her head. "What I really wanted was the constant reaffirmation of my own worth that life gave me." Her gaze met Damita's. "I wanted to show everyone that I had importance even though I'd started out as a whore."

"You weren't really a whore. You couldn't help—"

"I was a whore," Lola said clearly. "I sold myself. No matter what reasons I had for doing it, that fact remains. In a way I've been prostituting myself to an even greater extent since I gave up being a call girl. I think it's even worse to bargain with your beliefs than with your body."

Damita gazed at her mother with amazement. There was no question of Lola's sincerity. "You did it for me," she whispered. "You wanted to give me a good life."

"I thought so at the time. Now I'm not so sure. Maybe I wanted to grab the brass ring on a carousel that never stopped. I was poor and hungry and I wanted so many pretty things." Lola shook her head wearily. "Yet I wanted admiration and respect too. It could be that I painted a lovely picture of myself as a martyr so I could have both."

"No," Damita said fiercely. "You're not selfish. You're loving and kind."

"You've always envisioned me that way," Lola said gently. "I'm not unkind, but I was never a prize. And it's easy to love you, *querida*. You're so very loving yourself. Ever since you were a small child you've desperately wanted to love someone and you had only me."

"You've always been more than enough."

"No, I wasn't enough," Lola said sadly. "I didn't give you what you needed. I cheated you and I cheated myself of all those years of your childhood when we could have been together.'"

"You were trying to protect me."

"Or myself."

Damita swallowed to ease the painful tightening in her throat. "Why are you saying these things? You're not going to convince me you're some kind of villainess. I love you."

"Thank God," Lola said softly. "I don't deserve it, but I do thank God for it. I hope you'll keep on loving me, Damita. I'll try my best to earn your love in the future. But the reason I'm telling you all this isn't that I want forgiveness." She held up her hand as Damita opened her lips to protest. "In spite of what you say, I know I'll have to earn it. I just wanted to warn you that it's not easy to be honest with yourself but it's the only way to keep from making monumental mistakes."

"I don't know what you're trying to tell me."

Lola leaned forward and brushed Damita's cheek

with her lips. "Think about it, Damita. Do what I did. Tear down the lies you've been telling yourself all these years and start fresh. Think about me, think about Cam. And most of all, think about yourself. I believe you'll be surprised at some of the conclusions you come to." She turned and walked swiftly toward the door. As she opened the door she glanced back over her shoulder. "Promise me?"

"I promise," Damita said slowly.

Lola's loving smile lit her face. "I'll see you in London, *querida*. Take care."

Damita stared at the door a long time after it closed behind Lola. Then she turned and dropped onto one of the chairs at the rattan table. Her mother's words had stunned and completely bewildered her. Everything was topsy-turvy and nothing made sense. Beliefs she'd held for a lifetime were suddenly shifting and disappearing. She had to make order out of this chaos. She must think clearly and without deception as she had promised Lola she would.

Cam didn't arrive back at the line shack until almost midnight, but the candles were still burning and Damita was curled up on the bed reading a dog-eared paperback book.

She immediately laid the book aside when he appeared in the door. "Lola?"

"She's on her way. I saw the jet take off myself."

Cam closed the door. "She promised she'd have the authorities notify us as soon as they have her in one of their safe houses."

Damita felt a little of the tension ease out of her. "Thank heavens." She let out a long breath. "No sign of Belstrop's men?"

He shook his head. "No one tried to intercept us, but that doesn't necessarily mean no one was watching Half Moon. We may have moved too fast for them."

But Lola's safe?"

He nodded. "Lola's safe. She'll be in Scotland Yard's hands the minute she gets off the plane." He paused. "But the danger to you is correspondingly magnified now. Lola wanted to avoid having you share her danger, but it didn't occur to her how vulnerable you're going to be until you reach England. Since Lola's now out of reach, you're the only possible weapon Belstrop has to silence her." His lips tightened. "Which is why we're not going to wait until tomorrow to put you on that plane for London as your dear mother decreed. I'm driving you back to Sydney tonight. I've made reservations for us on the three A.M. flight and we'll—"

"No."

He went still. "What?"

She swung her feet to the floor and stood up. "I said no. The original arrangement stands; we leave tomorrow night."

"The hell we will," Cam said in a growl. "I've just told you why we—"

"Lola was right, you don't know if Half Moon is being watched. You don't even know if Belstrop knows I'm related to Lola." Damita met his gaze calmly. "It's a calculated risk I'm willing to take."

"Why take any risk at all?" Cam asked explosively. "Why stay here when it's safer for you to board the plane tonight?"

"Because we need this time. Isn't that the reason you told me you took me to Kasmara?"

Cam's brow wrinkled. "That was different. I didn't know Belstrop was trailing our footsteps then."

"You still don't know for sure he is." She moistened her lips with her tongue. "And I'm not going anyway. Not until I find out something very important to me."

"Find out what?"

She took a deep breath and then let it out in a little rush. "If I love you."

His eyes widened. "Damita—"

"And if you really love me." She rushed on. "You said you did before, but then after last night I thought you didn't, and I got confused and hurt and—"

"Damita, what the hell are you trying to say?"

"I thought I was saying it." Her hands clenched nervously at her sides. "Lola told me to think and be honest with myself and that's what I've been doing all these hours you've been gone." Her lips were trembling as she smiled at him. "It's not been the most pleasant time in my life. The fruits of honesty aren't all they're cracked up to be. For instance, I found out several less than pretty aspects to my character. I'm not a very nice person."

"I don't agree. You're loyal and sweet and—"

"We mustn't be looking in the same mirror," she interrupted. "I'm not sweet. I'm as prickly as the bramble bush you compared me to. I'm belligerent and frank to the point of rudeness. I did think I was at least honest, but I don't even have that virtue. I've been lying to myself about the most important person in my life."

"Lola?"

She nodded jerkily. "I was ashamed of her. I accepted her rejection of me because I didn't want to face being Lola Torres's daughter. I was so petty that I couldn't see . . ." She trailed off and swallowed to ease the painful tightness of her throat. "Maybe Lola even sensed the way I felt and it was the reason she decided not to let anyone know I was her daughter."

"You can't shoulder the blame for Lola's decisions, Damita. And you can't blame yourself for feeling the way you did as a child. The nuns gave you a set of values that made Lola's past difficult for you to accept."

"She blames herself, but I'm just as much to blame. We've both made so many mistakes," Damita whispered. "I love her, Cam."

"I know you do."

"And she loves me."

"Yes."

"I want to talk to her. I want to tell her I'm not going to be belligerent or defensive any longer. I'm going to tell her how stupid I've been and how proud I am she's my mother."

"Then, dammit, let's get on the plane tonight."

She shook her head. "I can't. Because there's a problem I have to solve here first." She took a step toward him. "I'm probably a mass of complexes and insecurities, but I'm going to try to climb over them and get to the bottom of this. Not easy for me. I've never really trusted in a man-woman relationship. I thought most men were users."

"Understandable, considering what you knew about Lola's life in the barrio." His lips twisted. "And I certainly didn't do anything to change your opinion."

She looked at him in surprise. "But you did. You're not like the men who forced Lola into that life, Cam. I tried to tell myself you were like them after last night, but I knew down deep it wasn't really true. Now I have to clear this up." She took a deep breath and then burst out, "Did I do something to turn you off last night?"

"No," he said huskily. "Hell no, you were—"

"Then why did you dump me and run for cover?" she asked bluntly. "I know it's not supposed to be physically terrific for a man to make love to a virgin, but I don't think your reaction was consistent with—"

"For God's sake, I practically raped you," he said harshly. "I promised myself I'd be patient and I broke that promise, dammit. You were a virgin and the one time I should have been gentle and given you time to become accustomed to me, I blew it. It's no wonder you couldn't respond to me."

"I didn't respond?" Damita gazed at him in bewilderment. "But I did respond. At least, I thought I did." She tried to think back, but she could remember only heat and fullness and wild passion. "I didn't know much about the subtleties of what we were doing, but it *felt* as if I were responding. I certainly wasn't fighting you."

"You didn't fight me," he agreed grimly. "And that's incredible considering I savaged you like an animal."

"You didn't savage me." The words were spoken abstractedly as she gazed at him intently. "You feel *guilty*?"

"You're damn right I feel guilty. I was going to be so blasted noble and then I got panicky and acted like a— Why are you laughing?"

"I think I'm relieved. I thought there was something wrong with me." A smile still lingered on her lips. "In fact, you were so cold this morning, I was sure of it."

"There wasn't anything wrong with you. It was *me*." He continued quickly. "But don't worry, once we reach England I'll give you plenty of time to become accustomed to me. I won't even touch you until you feel easier with me."

"You won't?" She gazed at him with a mixture

of exasperation and bemusement. "I don't remember telling you I felt uneasy with you."

"But you're confused and shaken now. You just told me so." He gazed at her with concern. "We probably shouldn't even be talking while you're in this state."

"I'm not in any kind of 'state,' and I'm no fragile little wimp who has to be coddled. You're underestimating me, dammit. Lola said we were both muddled, but I think you have the edge on me. It's a good thing I decided to stay here another day. Once we're surrounded by all those people in London, there's no telling what kind of misunderstandings you're capable of concocting."

"There won't be any misunderstandings." Cam's voice held a thread of its former grimness. "Just as soon as you're back on safe ground I'll begin handling everything slowly and methodically."

"*You'll* handle?" Damita shook her head. "Oh, no, this may be the most important decision of my life and I won't have it handled by you or anyone else." She suddenly bit her lower lip. "Oh, dear, that sounded belligerent, didn't it?"

He smiled. "Very."

"Well, you deserved it," she said defiantly. "You can't expect a complete reformation in the blink of an eye."

"I'd be disappointed if all your sharp edges disappeared. I've gotten to like your thorny exterior. It must be the masochist in me."

A rush of warmth like liquid sunshine rippled

through her. "You make me feel so . . . I've never felt anything like this before. It must mean I . . ." Her voice was only a level above a whisper. "Oh, I don't know. I guess I'm still pretty mixed up."

He stood there, waiting.

"But I want to find out." Her lips set determinedly. "I *will* find out. And we're not going anywhere until I do."

"No matter what I say or do?"

"We're staying."

"I should have known it was useless to argue with you." He smiled ruefully. "You're as stubborn as Lola."

"Like mother, like daughter," Damita quoted softly. "And I'm damned proud I'm like her. Since that's settled, we might as well make ourselves comfortable. Have you had anything to eat?"

"I grabbed a sandwich at the airport."

"Coffee? I think I've managed to conquer the eccentricities of that ancient monstrosity of a stove."

"It's after midnight. Neither of us will sleep if we dose ourselves with caffeine." He suddenly grew somber as his gaze fell on the bed against the wall. "Which brings up an interesting question. One single bed, two people."

"No problem." Her gaze slid away from him. "We'll share it."

"The hell we will," he said with soft vehemence.

Her gaze flew back to his face. "Why not? You said I didn't displease you. I've heard sex can twist emotions all out of shape, but I think it would be a good way to find out what I'm feeling toward you."

"Good Lord, you sound like a scientist dissecting a frog," Cam said with disgust.

He was angry, Damita realized. Cam's lips were a flat line in the tautness of his face, and his eyes were blazing at her. "I didn't mean to be analytical. I'm a little nervous, and that makes me clumsy with words. Why are you so upset with me?"

"I'm not upset with—" He stopped. "Hell yes, I'm upset. Do you think this is easy for me? I *want* you, dammit." His voice was hoarse. "I want to drag you down on that bed and plunge inside you. I want to watch your face when I move in and out. I want to—"

"Then do it." She could feel the color stain her cheeks as heat stormed through her. "I told you I thought it would be a good idea."

"That's not enough. I have to be sure it's right the next time." He gestured impatiently. "No quick tumbles. I cheated you. I won't cheat you again. You're entitled to all the trimmings, and by God you'll get them."

Her throat tightened as an aching tenderness swept through her, filling her with a sweet, wild joy. If this wasn't love, it was so close to it as to be almost indistinguishable. "You won't let me persuade you?"

He shook his head.

"Then may I ask where you're going to sleep?"

"I'll bring the jeep closer to the shack and bed down there." He turned away. "I'll see you in the morning."

She suddenly began to chuckle and he glanced back over his shoulder with a frown. "What's so funny?

"I was just thinking about all the thousands of beds in all those thousands of bedrooms in the hotels you own." Her eyes were dancing. "And now there's nary a place to lay your weary head."

"You don't have to be so blasted happy about it."

"I'm not happy. I think you're being a complete idiot about this. You deserve an uncomfortable night."

"Thanks." He opened the door. "I assure you I'll definitely have a miserable enough one to please even you."

Tenderness, exasperation, and that strange, poignant joy conflicted within her as she watched the door swing shut behind him. If Cam was behaving like an idiot, then she was no better. As a seductress she was definitely amateur status, saying all the wrong things and expressing herself as clumsily as a nitwit child. She had been unbearably touched by Cam's quixotic attitude and hadn't even let him see it. Her defenses had automatically risen to keep out the tide of emotion that had threatened to overwhelm her. Lord, she had even laughed at the possibility of his discomfort, she thought with profound self-disgust.

It was incredible he could bring himself to like, much less love her.

And she didn't think she could go on if Cam didn't love her.

The realization struck her with blinding suddenness and even more stunning force. Heaven help her, she *did* love him. Oh, dear, and he had said he cared for her, but how could he? She had shown him nothing but belligerence and brashness since the moment she had met him. He would have to be the masochist he had joked he was to find any pleasure in her company.

But she could change; she could learn to speak sweetly. She could cast off all her prickly thorns. She *would* change.

She began to undress, her gaze fixed absently on the flickering flames of the candles in the candelabra on the table. After all, it shouldn't be too difficult to smooth out most of her rough edges.

Not when she wanted to change so desperately.

Not when she loved Cam so desperately.

Eight

Damita moved swiftly through the brush, her tennis shoes nearly silent on the leaf-strewn path. Cam had said he would move the jeep closer, but it seemed as if she had been walking forever since she left the cabin. It probably hadn't been that far at all. Undoubtedly it was only because her nerves were so on edge that it seemed so—

"Stop right there!" Cam's voice had the stunning menace of a whiplash. The headlights of the jeep suddenly punched through the darkness, pinning her in place with their brilliant beam.

She heard Cam mutter a disgusted curse. "Good God, what are you doing out here?"

"Being scared out of my wits," she said tartly. "First you yell at me and then you try to blind me with those headlights." She held up a hand to shade her eyes. "Can't you turn them off?"

The lights were immediately doused and she breathed a sigh of relief. "That's better. I felt as if you were going to give me the third degree at any minute."

"I am." Cam's tone was grim. "What the devil are you doing wandering around in the woods? I'm out here trying to guard you from Belstrop's goons and you decide to leave the cabin for a midnight stroll. Don't you have any sense of self-preservation?"

She started toward the dim outline of the jeep. "I'm not strolling. Strolling indicates a certain aimlessness and I have a definite purpose in mind. As for self-preservation . . ." She stopped beside the driver's side of the jeep, trying to see Cam's expression, but it was too dark beneath the shadows formed by the trees to get more than an impression of almost palpable tension. "That's part of the purpose."

"Damita, this is no time for you to turn enigmatic."

She laughed shakily. "I've never been enigmatic in my life. I wouldn't know how. If anything, I've always been too up front for my own good. I've no intention of keeping anything hidden from you, Cam." She paused. "Nothing at all."

"It's too cool out here. Go back to the cabin."

"I'm not chilly. I want to talk to you."

"We can talk in the morning. There's been enough conversation between us for one night."

He sounded terribly tired, and Damita felt a sudden rush of tenderness. "Very well, we won't talk." She came around to the passenger side of the jeep and stepped into it. "I'll just sit here and keep you company." She leaned back against the seat. "It is a little chilly, isn't it? It was so balmy last night on the terrace that I guess I didn't expect it to be cool tonight."

"What in hell do you expect when you're traipsing around in nothing but a robe?" Cam said. "What are you trying to do to me, Damita? I told you I wasn't going to let you—" He broke off and drew a deep breath. "This isn't a game we're playing."

"I know." Damita's voice was uneven. "I've never been more serious in my life. And don't be so defensive, I'm not trying to seduce you. I wouldn't really know how to go about it. I simply want to be with you. I was lying there in bed and thinking about you and remembering what you said about having a miserable night and what a callous shrew you must have thought me."

Cam was silent, listening. She wished she could see his face. It would have made it easier to go on with this. "And I realized I didn't want to be lying in there in that comfortable bed if you were out here. I didn't want to be warm if you were cold, or full if you were hungry. I couldn't stand it. So I'll just sit here with you, and if you don't want to talk, that's fine. I don't really feel like talking either."

"For someone who doesn't want to talk, you're doing a lot of it," Cam said softly.

"That's because I'm nervous. I always talk a lot when I'm nervous. When I was a little girl, Lola used to say no one could get a word out of me unless I was nervous, and then I wouldn't shut up."

"What made you nervous?"

"Oh, lots of things. When I wasn't sure I did well on a test or if one of the sisters acted as if she were displeased with me. And I was always nervous when I knew Lola was coming." She paused, surprised. "You know, I never realized that before. About Lola, I mean. I always thought I was excited, but I was nervous as well. She was always so beautiful and clever, and everyone tried to please her. I guess I was worried about pleasing her too." She stopped, and when she spoke again, her voice was a mere whisper. "And now I worry about pleasing you, Cam."

"You do please me." He sat hunched over the wheel, his hands tightly grasping the steering wheel. "Oh, hell!" Then he was pulling her into his arms, pressing her head against his chest with rough tenderness. "And I'm not going to give you any tests or make you feel . . ." He stopped, but his hand was infinitely gentle as it stroked her hair. He repeated huskily, "You do please me, Damita."

"Good." She nestled closer. "I didn't mean to sound melodramatic. I had a very nice childhood really."

"You've said that before."

"Well, it's true." She shifted on the seat. "Lord, these seats are hard."

"Jeeps aren't known for their luxurious upholstery."

"I don't know how you thought you could get any rest at all camped out here."

"It wasn't the hardness of the seats that I was afraid would keep me awake," he said dryly. "I haven't slept more than a few hours since you burst into my hotel room."

"Well, you would have had a better chance in the bed in the cabin than out here. I can't see why you're being so stupid. You should—" She broke off. "Oh, hell, I did it again. Stop laughing, blast you."

"I can't help it." She could hear the laughter reverberating in Cam's chest beneath her ear. "I don't know why you're trying so hard to become something you're not. I like Damita Shaughnessy exactly the way she is."

"Then you're crazy as a loon," she said crossly. She heard the rumble of his laughter begin once again and sighed resignedly. "There, you see? I've called you stupid and crazy in the space of a minute. I'd say there's definite room for improvement."

"But on the plus side, you left your bed to come

and keep me company. And you're letting me touch you and hold you." His hand continued to stroke her hair. "Did I ever tell you how nice you are to hold? You're sort of cuddly and comforting."

"You make me sound like a dog-eared teddy bear," she grumbled.

"I assure you a teddy bear never had this effect on me."

"Well, I think I'm getting more out of this than you are." She suddenly straightened. "And I don't want to do that, dammit. I'm here to do just the opposite. You're always giving to someone else, and I decided I wanted to give to you this time. I can be a port in a storm too. Try me."

"I'd be delighted. There's only one problem."

"What's that?"

"You *are* the storm, luv." Then he broke into laughter again and began to rock her back and forth. "I'll make a deal with you. We'll take turns being the safety net, okay?"

His arms were strong and his heart a steady throb beneath her ear. Damita felt joy pour through her in a sweet golden stream. "No, it's not okay." Her voice was muffled against him. "You've taken enough turns with Damon and Lola and heaven only knows how many other people I don't know about."

His lips feathered her temple. "Who's counting?"

"I am. But don't worry, I'll think of a way to balance the scales."

"And how do you intend to do that?" Cam asked.

Give gifts to a giver of gifts, comfort to the comforter, sunlight to the sun. "Never mind." Her arms tightened lovingly around him. "We'd better try to go to sleep. Though heaven knows how we'll do it on these hard, lumpy seats."

It was Damita who drifted off to sleep first over an hour later. Cam's arms automatically tightened around her as her breathing slowed and she relaxed against him with the boneless contentment of a kitten. It was incredible to him that she could sleep so soundly under these conditions, but she had told him the first night at the hotel in Marasef she always slept soundly. Lord, that night seemed long ago, he mused. They had both learned so much in such a short time about themselves and about each other.

He had never dreamed he was capable of the complexity of emotions he was experiencing now. His body was ready, even hurting, with a purely sensual hunger, and yet there was also this warm glow of tenderness. He smiled as he remembered how denigratingly Damita had referred to herself as a teddy bear. She wouldn't be at all pleased to realize the concept had struck a chord within him. She did remind him of a teddy bear. There was something wonderfully magical about teddy bears. They were beloved companions to hold through the night, friends to share the tears and joys of childhood, and still remained a glowing memory even after childhood had passed.

Damita stirred against him and murmured.

The night breeze was sharpening, the chill increasing. Damita shouldn't be out here, he thought with sudden anxiety. Her silk robe was too thin, and he should have insisted she go back to the cabin. He smiled ruefully at the thought. He knew damn well she wouldn't have left him even if he had insisted. She had a crazy idea she had to share his discomfort. Crazy but sweet and unbearably touching.

And he knew she wouldn't leave him if he woke her and told her to go back now.

Which left only one solution, he thought resignedly.

She was being carried, Damita realized drowsily. Where were they going? Not that it mattered as long as she could feel the comforting throb of Cam's heart beneath her ear. Nothing could be very wrong as long as she was secure in Cam's arms. Yet perhaps she should rouse herself to ask him. "Cam, where—?"

"Shh. It's all right." He was placing her carefully on a bed. Sudden uneasiness surged through her. It was all too familiar. "You said that before." she opened lids heavy with sleep. "But it wasn't. You went away . . ."

"I had to go." He pulled off her tennis shoes and dropped them on the floor.

"Don't go away now," she whispered.

"I won't." His deep blue eyes were glowing in the candlelight.

"Good." Her lids fluttered closed. "I'd have to follow you and I'm so tired."

"Would you?" His voice was husky. "That's good to know." He lay down beside her and gathered her into his arms. "But you don't have to worry tonight. I'm not going anywhere. Just relax. I'm here and I'm going to stay here." His lips brushed the tip of her nose. "You can pretend I'm your very favorite teddy bear."

He was very much here, she thought contentedly as she sank back into the warm darkness. He was a solid, shining presence holding back the night. What else had he said? Oh, yes, something about a teddy bear. . . .

The first gray light of dawn was pouring through the windows when Damita woke. She opened her eyes drowsily and then came abruptly awake. Cam. Beside her. Asleep.

She gazed down at him and felt a warm rush of tenderness. Cam's dark brown hair was tousled, and he looked younger, more vulnerable now than she'd ever seen him. Yet there were deep lines of strain around his lips even in sleep.

She was the cause of that strain, she thought with remorse. She had gone to offer comfort but she had been aware that he wanted her last night in the jeep. Then to cap it off she had fallen asleep and he had been forced by his innate sense of gallantry to put her to bed and lie beside her all through the night.

No, he hadn't been forced, she thought with affectionate exasperation. He could have made love to her if he hadn't gotten it into his head he owed her some kind of compensation.

All the trimmings, he had said. What the devil would he consider all the trimmings? Candlelight, a romantic atmosphere, flowers . . .

She stiffened as a thought occurred to her. Why shouldn't she be the one to decide? He obviously didn't know what was good for him or he wouldn't be lying here looking so strained and tense. Perhaps there was some way she could satisfy his sense of what was due her and still give him what he needed.

She edged across the narrow bed, moving slowly, careful not to awaken him. Then she was on her feet and tightening the belt of her robe. She picked up her tennis shoes from the floor and glided silently toward the front door.

It would obviously have to be a two-pronged attack, she thought, her brow wrinkling in concentration. Cam was so determined to be chivalrous. She slowly opened the door. The hinges squeaked and her gaze flew to the bed across the room.

Cam didn't stir.

She breathed a sigh of relief and with utmost caution closed the door behind her.

• • •

"Wake up, Cam."

Cam opened his eyes to see Damita smiling down at him. She was still wearing the navy blue robe and tennis shoes she had worn last night, but her hair was freshly brushed and he caught the clean scent of soap.

She held out a steaming mug of coffee as she sat down on the bed beside him. "I just made it. Take a sip. It will wake you up before you jump into the shower." She made a face. "Not that the shower itself won't wake you up. There's no hot water."

"I know. No generator. It was one of Lola's biggest complaints." He took the mug and lifted it to his lips, gazing at her over the rim. "You look bright-eyed and alert this morning."

Damita looked more than alert, he thought. Her cheeks were flushed as if she had a fever, and her dark eyes were blazing. Maybe she did have fever, he thought with concern. She had been wandering around in the cool night air last night. "Do you feel okay?"

Damita nodded vigorously. "I feel wonderful." She jumped up and walked back toward the stove, keeping her back to him. "I've never felt better in my life. Go take your shower. I want to go for a walk. I was out earlier, and there seem to be all sorts of interesting wildflowers in these woods."

"You seem to have already gathered all the available ones in the neighborhood." His gaze circled the room as he swung his feet to the floor. There were flowers everywhere. Not only were all the vases overflowing with fresh flowers but Damita had filled drinking glasses, bowls, and cups until they brimmed with a symphony of pink, yellow, and cream-colored blossoms. "Why so many?"

Damita didn't look at him as she poured herself a cup of coffee. "I like flowers." She cradled the cup in her hands. "Hurry."

"I'm on my way." He stood up and took a final sip of coffee before striding across the room toward the tiny bathroom. He set his cup on the rattan table as he passed. "Ten minutes."

The door closed behind him and a moment later Damita heard the water in the shower.

Her hands were trembling around the coffee mug, she noticed. Not that it surprised her, when she felt as if every muscle in her body were quaking with a force that would have registered eight on the Richter scale. She drew a steadying breath and closed her eyes. Count to five, she told herself, repeating the prescription for nervousness she had doctored herself with when she was a child. When she reached five, everything would be fine and she wouldn't be nervous anymore. One, two, three—

Her eyes flicked open with sudden impatience with herself. The prescription wasn't going to work now any more than it had then. There wasn't any magic in it. She just had to brace herself and do what was necessary.

She set her coffee cup down with a resounding

click on the table and marched toward the bathroom, untying her robe as she went. She threw open the door, jerked out of her robe, and let it fall to the floor.

She opened the door of the shower stall and froze, staring at him.

Cam's eyes widened. "Damita, what the hell—?"

The spray sheened the powerful muscles of his naked body. He looked tough, virile, and so blasted beautiful, she started to shake again. Then she was in the tiny cubicle with him, the cold spray hitting her with needlelike force. Despair suddenly shattered her fragile control. She wasn't going to be able to pull this off. How could you expect a man to become aroused when he was being deluged with icy water? Why hadn't she remembered the reason men took cold showers? "I was trying to seduce you, dammit." She threw her arms around him and buried her face in the springy hair thatching his chest. "Only the water is ice cold instead of warm, and I look terrible with wet hair, and I'm scared to death." Tears were running down her cheeks. "And you're stubborn as a jackass and probably wouldn't want me anyway."

Then she noticed something else and her voice rose in an exasperated wail. "And I forgot to take off my tennis shoes!"

He gazed down at her dumbfounded and then started to laugh helplessly.

"Stop laughing. It's not funny."

"I can't stop." He opened the shower door and stepped out of the stall. "I think I'm hysterical." He pulled her out of the shower stall. "You've finally pushed me over the boundary between reason and insanity." He jerked a towel from the towel rack and dried himself sketchily before wrapping it around her head and reaching for another towel. He began to dry her with impersonal thoroughness, as if she were a small child, running the soft terry cloth over her shoulders, her breasts, her bottom. Then he tied the towel around her in a sarong, tucking the ends securely at her breasts. "Listen to me, Damita. This was—"

"No." She wiped her eyes with the back of her hand. "I have no intention of listening to you when you don't make any sense." She whirled and marched out of the bathroom. "Come here, I want to show you something."

"Damita. . ." He followed her slowly into the room.

Her eyes blazed at him. "You said you wanted me to have trimmings." She punched her finger toward a vase on the bureau overflowing with flowers. "I have trimmings. There are more flowers in here than there are in some flower shops. And we could have candlelight, except that it's daylight and that would be pretty silly. What other trimmings could I want? Can't you see how stupid you're being?"

He frowned. "It's not the same."

"Because you didn't bring them to me? Did you ever think that maybe I'd like to do things for you too? I've never had anyone to give presents to. Why shouldn't I be the one to give you all these trimmings you're so high on?"

"Because I owe you—"

"The devil you do. You don't owe me anything. Let's get that straight. I'm sorry I wasn't as responsive as you would have liked, but I enjoyed what happened between us. Do you understand? You probably would have realized how much I was enjoying it if you hadn't been so concerned about my freezing up on you at Kasmara."

His lips tightened. "You're wrong. I was incapable of noticing anything when I made love to you. All I could think of was how much I wanted you."

"Well, so what? I liked that too."

Surprise replaced the frown on his face. "You did?"

She nodded. "You told me it was right, remember? It *was* right, Cam. It wouldn't have been right at Kasmara because I wanted you but I didn't really trust you and I had this thing about being used. So you immediately jumped to the conclusion I had a whole bagful of complexes I'd carried over from my so-called deprived childhood." She took a deep breath. "The only thing you got right was when you said you cheated me. You did cheat me, but not the way you think."

His gaze was suddenly intent. "No?"

"No, it was afterward that you cheated me. I wanted to be held and made to feel loved, and you left me alone to imagine all kinds of nonsense."

Her eyes were once more glittering with tears. "It was the only time I felt cheated or used. When you left me—"

"Don't cry," he said hoarsely. "For God's sake, don't cry."

"I'll cry if I feel like it." She wiped her eyes again with the back of her hand. "And I definitely feel like it. I'm standing here looking terrible, with red eyes and soggy tennis shoes, and I wanted everything to be so beautiful."

"It is beautiful," Cam said gently. "You're beautiful, Damita."

"No, I'm— what are you doing?"

His hand clasped her wrists and he was pulling her across the room. "I'm trying to make amends."

"Haven't you been listening to me? I don't want you to make amends. You don't need—"

"Will you be quiet, luv?" Cam asked. "We obviously need to reach a compromise that will satisfy us both." He pushed her gently down on the bed and knelt to take off her wet tennis shoes. His voice lowered to velvet softness. "One we'll both enjoy."

"You mean . . ." Damita felt the air leave her lungs. "You're not doing this because you feel sorry for me?"

"No." He smiled ruefully. "I'm afraid I'm doing this because I feel sorry for me." With a flip of his finger at her breast he loosened the towel and it fell to her waist. "So much for being noble."

"You are noble," she said quickly. "And kind and—"

"Hurting," he finished for her, his gaze on the fullness of her naked breasts. "Oh, how I'm hurting, Damita."

"I don't want you to hurt," she whispered. "Not ever. Can't we do something about it?"

He sat down beside her. "I believe we're about to." He lifted her onto his lap and cuddled her close, his palm caressing her back, running from her shoulder blades to the base of her spine. "And soon. I don't think I can wait much longer."

"Neither can I." The hardness of his hand on her flesh was sending streaks of fire with every stroke. She started to close her eyes and let the waves of pleasure wash over her. Then she realized what she was doing and sat up abruptly. "No, let me." She turned around so that she was astraddle him. "I want to help. I want to bring you pleasure this time." Her fingertips lightly caressed his chest and shoulders. "Do you like this?"

His muscles tensed beneath her touch. "Yes," he said thickly.

She moved closer until the tips of her breasts were brushing against him with every breath she took. She didn't know how long she could continue with this. She felt as if she had a fever, and she could feel the tingles growing between her thighs where the center of her womanhood was pressing against his arousal. Her head slowly lowered. "I want to taste you." Her tongue licked delicately at his left nipple.

She felt a shudder go through him and looked up to see his nostrils flaring as his breathing became harsh.

"Salty." She licked again. "But I think I like it."

"I know I do." His hand tangled in the towel on her hair and he pulled it off before pressing her mouth to his body. He shuddered again as her teeth closed gently on his flesh. "It's too much, Damita."

"Just a little more." She slid still closer and heard the sharp intake of his breath. "I want to please you. I want you to enjoy yourself."

"If I . . . enjoy myself . . . any more, it's going to *kill* me." His fingers tightened in her hair. "Damita, I can't . . . stand this. I'm going crazy. Please . . ."

She lifted her head. "If you're sure—" She broke off. Fullness. Delight. Cam. Her fingernails dug into his shoulders as he started a rhythm that was so wild it reached to her very depths.

"Oh, I'm sure." His words were groaned between clenched teeth. "I couldn't be more sure."

Neither could she, Damita thought hazily. Nothing could be more certain than this beautiful *rightness*. Passion, warmth, safety. They were all here in Cam's arms, and she wanted it to go on forever.

The rhythm was accelerating, the strokes deepening, the warmth growing.

"Damita, please," Cam gasped. "Tell me it's all right. I can't hold on."

"Then don't . . . Don't . . . Her hands clutched mindlessly at his shoulders as the pleasure mounted to an unbearable pitch. "Cam, I want—"

The rapture was so sharp it was close to pain. Wave after wave of pleasure exploded through her with exquisite force.

She collapsed against him, her cheek on his chest. His heart was still thundering, she noticed through the veil of exhaustion that was clouding her senses. What a lovely, powerful sound.

Then Cam was lifting her off him onto the bed. She made a low murmur of protest. "No . . . I don't want to leave you."

"Neither do I." Cam's lips brushed her temple. "But we can't stay this way indefinitely." He lay down beside her and drew her into his arms with great tenderness. "Not that it wouldn't be pleasant. However, with that kind of provocation we'd soon be engaged in the same activity we've just concluded."

"What's wrong with that?"

"You said I cheated you before when I left you. I think I'd be cheating you again if we made love right now. You want to be cuddled, so we cuddle." He lifted her chin to kiss her with sweetness. "I'm not usually so stupid about these things. It's just that what I feel for you has me turned inside out."

"Oh, Cam . . ." She had to stop as her throat tightened with unbearable tenderness. "I think you must be a throwback to some other era. You have to be descended from a very long line of impossibly chivalrous gentlemen. Didn't anyone ever tell you that being as nice as this went out with high button shoes?"

"So I'm old-fashioned. If that's what you want, then you're entitled to it." He drew her closer, his fingers stroking her hair. "And besides, I like it too. You're just the right size for me to cuddle."

"Am I?" Her eyes closed to hide their mistiness as she nestled closer to him. He was just the right size for her too, she thought. In heart as well as body, in glowing warmth of spirit as well as passion. "I'd say we're a pretty good match." Her lips brushed his shoulder lovingly. "In fact, a very good match."

Nine

Damon descended on the line shack like an exploding volcano three hours later.

"Have you seen him?" He strode into the cabin and slammed the door behind him. "I left two men at Half Moon to interrogate your people and seek out any of his men he might have planted there. Where's Lola?"

Cam quickly pulled the sheet up to cover Damita before raising himself on one elbow. "Good afternoon, Damon," he said dryly. "How nice of you to knock."

"I forgot." Damon gestured impatiently. "Do you want me to observe the amenities?" He bowed politely to Damita. "How delightful to see you again, Damita. You look quite ravishing without your clothes. You have—" He broke off as he caught

Cam's fierce expression. "Well, she does. Damita undresses exceptionally well. Before you pulled up the sheet I noticed that she has truly magnificent . . ." He stopped, and a faint smile tugged at his lips. "Shoulders."

Damita pulled the sheet higher around her neck before sitting up. "Hello, Damon."

"I see you've decided to be accommodating," he said approvingly. "Did he please you?"

"Damon." Cam said warningly.

"Well, I didn't ask her if she pleased you." Damon's eyes were twinkling. "I was tempted, but that would have been terribly chauvinistic and I know Damita doesn't approve of—"

"Why are you here?" Cam interrupted.

"Belstrop, of course. I told you I was coming." Damon's smile vanished as his lips tightened grimly. "What have you been doing since you arrived here besides the obvious?"

"Damon, has anyone ever told you that you're outrageous?" Damita asked.

Damon didn't turn his gaze from Cam's face. "Frequently. I've learned to ignore it." He asked again, "Where's Lola?"

"She should be safe under lock and key by this time. She left for London yesterday. Damita and I leave in a few hours to join her."

"She's not here? I thought perhaps Belstrop might have found out where Lola was hiding." Damon's eyes narrowed thoughtfully. "He left London surreptitiously yesterday evening en route to Sydney. It doesn't make sense."

Cam went still. "How do you know he left London?"

"I told you I wanted him," Damon said coldly. "I took the precaution of notifying a private investigating firm I use on occasion to keep watch on him. There was a message waiting for me when I reached Sydney this morning that he left London from a private airport outside the city. I thought he'd received word that Lola was at Half Moon."

"Or that she had left Half Moon and was out of reach of his men," Cam said slowly.

"Then why would he bother to come halfway around the world at a time like this?"

"Damita. Belstrop must have discovered Damita is Lola's daughter. We moved too fast for Belstrop's men to intercept Lola, and his only chance now is to get hold of Damita to use as a club over her head."

"Good," Damon said with satisfaction. "Then we'll have him."

"Good?" Cam echoed incredulously. "I just told you Damita was a target."

"Then we'll protect her," Damon said. "But we'll keep her here until Belstrop shows and get Belstrop too."

"Damon!" Cam gazed at him in exasperation. "Let the authorities get Belstrop. It's Damita's safety that's important."

Damon frowned. "Why are you arguing with me? You know I have to get Belstrop."

"Let me put this in terms you understand." Cam touched Damita's bare shoulder with blatant possession before continuing slowly, as if speaking to a small child. "*Mine.* Mine to protect. Mine to care for. And you, the El Zabor, Belstrop, and Scotland Yard can all go to hell. Understood?"

Damon's face clouded. "Rosol was hurt and—"

"Mine," Cam repeated, enunciating even more clearly.

Damon glared at him for an instant. Then his lips began to twitch and he threw back his head and laughed. "Have it your own way."

"That's my intention," Cam said calmly. "Now, will you get the hell out of here so Damita can dress? I want to get her on that plane for London."

"I can't stay and watch?" Damon's eyes wandered over the sheet covering Damita's breasts. "Pity."

"Out."

"All right, all right. Don't get testy. Here's the plan. You can take her to London, but we form an escort for you until she's safe in Scotland Yard's hands." Damon turned to leave. "Get dressed. I'll wait outside and give instructions to my men."

"How many men did you bring?" Damita asked.

"Twenty-four."

Damita's eyes widened. "Good heavens, that's an army."

"They insisted." Damon shrugged. "They won't

be needed, but it's a tribal matter, so I let them come."

"We won't be able to get them all on the helicopter," Cam said. "And I sent Lola on the company jet, so we're taking the commercial flight from Sydney."

"I rented my own helicopter." Damon opened the door. "And my Learjet is waiting at a small private terminal at the Sydney airport. I'll cancel your reservations and take you to London myself. It will be much safer for Damita."

"Why do I feel you're snapping your fingers again?" Damita asked warily.

Damon smiled. "Because I am," he said softly. "There are times when being a barbarian can be very convenient." The door closed behind him.

"Hurry." Cam swung his feet to the floor and stood up. "Let's get out of here."

"Why should we rush so?" Damita slipped from the bed and moved toward the bathroom. "No one's going to get through the army Damon has parked out there."

"Unless he chooses to send his army away to make you seem a more vulnerable target."

"He'd do that?" Damita picked up the robe from the floor of the bathroom and slipped into it. "But he said he'd protect me."

"And he will." Cam was dressing quickly. "But in his own way, damn him. Belstrop's men hurt Rosol, and Damon intends to get his pound of flesh no matter what I say."

"Who's Rosol?" Damita opened the top drawer of the bureau and took out her underthings. "And why is Damon here anyway?"

"Belstrop's men tried to persuade Rosol, one of Damon's servants, to give them information about us. Rosol ended up in the hospital."

"Oh, no," Damita whispered. "Why didn't you tell me?"

"Would it have done any good?" Cam finished buttoning his shirt. "I knew it would only upset you, and it wasn't as if you could do anything to help after the fact."

"No wonder Damon wants Belstrop," she said slowly. "Maybe he's right. Maybe I should stay until—"

"No," he said sharply. "We're going."

"But Damon thinks—"

"I doubt if Damon is thinking at all right now. He's so furious, he's operating on automatic. Two of Damon's chief characteristics are possessiveness and his belief in revenge. All the education and civilizing influences in the world haven't been able to eliminate those emotions in him, and Belstrop managed to tap into both of them. If I didn't want to strangle Belstrop myself, I'd feel sorry for the bastard."

"I don't feel sorry for him," Damita said fiercely. "He wants to hurt Lola."

"Lola's safe. It's you we have to worry about." Cam had finished dressing and turned toward the door. "I'll be right outside. I have to talk to

Damon. I just remembered something he said when he came in."

"What?"

"That his men were interrogating my people at Half Moon. I've got to make sure that he didn't give them permission to use methods that were less than civilized." He opened the door and stopped as he glanced back at her over his shoulder. "Hell and damnation!" He slammed the door again and strode across the room toward her. "I didn't want it to be like this." He pulled her into his arms and kissed her. Hot, sweet, and hard. "I wanted it to be so damn good for you. I wanted it to be perfect." He kissed her again, and before she had a chance to speak, he had released her and was once again moving quickly across the room. "I knew I shouldn't have given in and listened to you." The door slammed behind him.

Damita stood gazing bemusedly at the door. Cam and his blasted obsession about what was due her. She shook her head as she began to dress. She wished he had given her a chance to tell him that nothing could have been more beautiful than the hours they had just spent together— though she, too, wished they'd had more time. There were so many things they still had to do and say to each other.

She hadn't even had a chance to tell Cam how much she loved him.

• • •

"Engine trouble?" Cam gazed at Damon suspiciously. "Since when do any of your planes ever have engine trouble? Your mechanics seem to believe that keeping your planes in perfect condition is their holy mission."

"Parts wear out," Damon said blandly. "I'm sure it won't take long to repair the Learjet. You and Damita can relax in the waiting room of the terminal until we're ready to leave Sydney. I've had my men clear it of all the employees so you can have privacy."

Cam's grasp tightened on Damita's arm. "I don't like this, Damon."

"You don't trust me?" Damon pretended to be hurt. "When have I ever betrayed your trust, Cam."

"I trust you to do exactly what you want to do. I saw you in a huddle with your men at Half Moon before we took off in the helicopter. What did they tell you?"

"Something very interesting. Belstrop did have men at Half Moon." Damon smiled. "But they won't bother you anymore."

"What did you do to—" Damita broke off. She wasn't sure she wanted to know. Damon's smile held a joyous savagery that made her distinctly uneasy. "I think Cam's right. I'm not sure I trust you either, Damon." She turned to go into the small terminal. "We'll give your mechanics fifteen minutes to get the plane fixed. Then we'll go to the main terminal and catch a commercial flight."

Surprise and then respect flitted across Damon's

face. He gave her a half-mocking salute. "Yes, ma'am. I'll give my mechanics your ultimatum." He turned away.

"Damon," Cam called.

Damon glanced back over his shoulder. "Yes?"

"There had better not be any trouble."

Damon shrugged. "Who knows when trouble will strike? One must learn to accept and deal with it." Then he was striding across the runway toward a sleek white jet with the name El Zabor inscribed in bold gold letters on the fuselage.

"I have an idea Damon knows very well when trouble will strike," Cam muttered. He turned on his heel and followed Damita into the terminal building. "And I don't believe we'll give him that fifteen minutes. I'm going to call Qantas and see if we can reinstate our reservations."

"I'll do it." Damita moved toward the telephone on the ticket desk across the room. Then she stopped short as she remembered something. "I can't go on Qantas."

"Why not?"

"Damon asked me to give him my passport before we left Half Moon. He said he'd smooth our way through immigration. Didn't he ask for yours?"

"No." Cam's lips thinned. "He knew damn well I'd smell a rat. He's up to something. I don't know how the hell he managed it, but I'd swear he's found a way to get what he wants."

"Belstrop," Damita whispered. "What are we going to do?"

"You stay here. I'm going out to the Learjet and make Damon give me your passport. Even if I have to strangle him to get it." He turned and moved toward the glass doors of the entrance. "Whatever you do, don't leave the terminal."

He was halfway across the tarmac when he saw the heavy rear door of the jet being thrown open and Damon appear abruptly in the doorway. A fierce scowl darkened the sheikh's face as he watched Cam stalking toward the plane. "Go back to the terminal, dammit, you're going to ruin everything."

"I want Damita's passport. And don't give me any excuses about misplacing it or—"

"Get back there." Damon's voice held a steely edge. "I've planned everything down to the least detail to keep Damita safe and I won't have you putting her in danger."

"*Me* put her in danger?" Cam drew a deep breath and tried to steady his temper. "You're the one who's putting her head on the block."

Damon shrugged. "I've taken advantage of the circumstances only to draw Belstrop into the open."

"What circumstances?"

"My men rooted out the men Belstrop planted at Half Moon." Damon smiled grimly. "Then they persuaded them to phone Belstrop and tell him Damita would be taking off from this terminal." He held up his hand as Cam started to swear beneath his breath. "I've taken every precaution. I've had the terminal searched and my men are watching the front gate and all the surrounding hangars. I'm watching the terminal myself from here. The minute we see anyone enter the terminal, we move in. Everything is covered." He frowned. "However, I wanted someone with her in the terminal itself. You were supposed to be inside to protect her just in case he—"

"Damn you!" Then Cam was whirling, tearing across the tarmac at a dead run toward the terminal building.

He could see Damita through the glass doors. She was standing quite still, her stance oddly rigid, her gaze on something out of his range of vision. Belstrop? Sick terror chilled him. Lord, don't let it be Belstrop.

He pushed open the glass doors.

"No!" Damita's gaze flew toward him. "Get out, Cam. Hurry."

"Come in, Mr. Bandor." The man standing beside the ticket counter gestured with the gun in his hand. "Pay no attention to the lady. I'm very glad you're here. You've caused me no end of trouble in the last two months, and I'll enjoy exacting compensation." The man's voice was rich, fruity, and very British public school. "I suppose you know who I am?"

"Belstrop," Cam said tersely.

"Correct."

"He was hiding in one of the toilet stalls in the bathroom, Cam," Damita said.

"A place in which he'd feel wonderfully comfortable, considering—"

"Don't say it, Mr. Bandor." Belstrop's hand tightened on the gun. "I'm already quite irritated with you for keeping Lola hidden from my men for so long. Now the three of us are going on a journey to a house I've rented on the edge of town. Then the enchanting Miss Shaughnessy is going to make a call to her bitch of a mother."

"I don't even know where she is," Damita said.

"Then I'm sure she'll try to contact you shortly." Belstrop smiled unpleasantly. "And will be quite concerned when she's unable to do so. That will be a message in itself, won't it?"

"Your plan won't work, Belstrop." Cam took a step forward.

The gun immediately swung to cover Cam. "Stay where you are, Mr. Bandor."

"Cam, please don't move." Damita looked at the gun. "You don't need Cam, Belstrop, leave him here."

"Be quiet, Damita," Cam said curtly. "You're not going anywhere without me."

"Don't tell me to be quiet." Damita's eyes blazed at him. "This is my life and my problem. Stay out of it. Let's go, Belstrop."

"My word. She obviously has the potential of being as much of a bitch as her mother." Belstrop's lips twisted. "Our time together may be more enjoyable than I thought. I might decide to see if she also shares Lola's more interesting talents. We spent many pleasurable hours together before she decided to bolt."

"According to Lola, the pleasure was entirely yours," Damita said acidly. "I believe the phrase she used was *'Quel ennui.'* "

Cam inhaled sharply. "Damita, for heaven's sake, this isn't the time to turn belligerent. The man's holding a gun on you."

"Very good advice." Belstrop's tone was laden with frost. He motioned toward the door with the gun. "Shall we go?"

Damita hesitated and then moved reluctantly toward the door.

"You too, Bandor," Belstrop said.

"No!" Damita whirled to face Belstrop. "It's stupid of you to take Cam when you don't need him. I'll go with you, but he stays."

Cam tensed to spring as he saw Belstrop's face flush with anger.

"Move!" Belstrop snarled.

"Not unless you promise to leave Cam here."

"Shut up!" Cam hissed. He could visualize a bullet tearing into Damita at any second. He grabbed her arm and propelled her forcefully toward the entrance. "We're both going."

A moment later they were outside the terminal with Belstrop trailing only a few feet behind.

"Straight ahead toward the gate," Belstrop ordered. "And I don't want any— What the—!"

A pistol shot rang out.

Damita! Cam cast a frantic glance at Damita, but she appeared unhurt and was gazing at him with the same concern and confusion he was feeling.

Cam whirled to see Belstrop struggling with Damon on the ground.

"Grab him," Damon yelled. "I can't hold him."

With lightning speed Cam covered the three steps separating him from the two struggling men. The side of his hand came down on Belstrop's neck in a karate chop.

Belstrop stiffened, groaned, then collapsed.

Cam gazed down at him numbly. It was over. Damita was safe. "What a stupid grandstand play, Damon. Where are all those dozens of men of yours?"

"When I followed you to the terminal and saw Belstrop holding a gun on you, I thought a one-man attack might have a better chance of success. I didn't want to risk Belstrop getting trigger happy."

"*Now* you worry about risk, after almost getting Damita killed." Cam's tone was bitter. "I think there's every possibility I may draw and quarter you."

"How unkind. And when I've shed my illustrious blood for your sake."

"Blood?" Cam's gaze shifted to where Damon was kneeling on the ground.

Damita ran forward. "Cam, he's been shot."

A great crimson stain was blossoming on the front of the sheikh's white shirt. Damon's lips were set with pain, and his bronze skin was now a shade paler than usual. "Only a trifling wound—" He stopped, and it was a moment before he could go on. He smiled unsteadily at Damita and tried to lift his right hand. "A wound no . . . more serious than a snap . . . of my fingers."

And he promptly pitched forward in a dead faint.

Ten

Damon looked as exotically out of place in the sterile white bed as a panther in a house-cat show, and, when Damita walked into the hospital room, the thin, gray-haired nurse standing beside the bed whirled to face her as if Damita were another panther invading her domain. "Who are you?" the nurse asked suspiciously. "It doesn't matter. You'll have to leave. Sheikh El Karim can't have any strenuous activity. I told him that and there'll be no arguments. Do you understand?"

"Certainly." Damita frowned anxiously. "I didn't realize his condition was so critical. Will talking tire him?"

"Talking?" the nurse echoed in bewilderment. "You only want to *talk* to him?"

"Come in, Damita." Damon scowled moodily at

the nurse. "This charming Florence Nightingale is the head nurse, Miss Adams. Pay no attention to her. There's just been a little misunderstanding."

"I can come back later."

Damon shook his head. "Stay." He punched his index finger at the nurse. "You go."

The nurse's lips set. "I'm staying in the room."

"We don't need a chaperone," Damon added silkily. "Or would you rather I call one of my men in the hall and have him carry you out?"

The nurse flushed with anger and whirled on her heel. "You don't run this hospital. I'm going to get an orderly to clear those savages out of the corridor."

"I wouldn't if I were you." Damon smiled tigerishly. "Or I'll yell with pain the next time you give me a shot, and you'll see what kind of reaction that brings from those 'savages.' "

The nurse's eyes widened in alarm, and she hurried from the room

"How peculiar." Damita crossed the room to stand by the bed. "Is she always that protective?"

"It's a misunderstanding," Damon repeated. "She thought you were a *kadin*.'"

"What?"

Damon looked a little uncomfortable. "Unfortunately, she walked into the room at a delicate moment yesterday." His lips twisted. "Exceptionally delicate."

"You had a *kadin* in here?"

"Two of them actually. But it's not as if I'd

summoned them," Damon said defensively. "And I wasn't doing anything strenuous. I was just letting them—" He frowned. "I don't see anything amusing. It was most frustrating."

Damita shook her head, trying vainly to smother the laughter that persisted in welling up. "You've been in here only two days, and you needed the services of a *kadin*? That wound mustn't have been as serious as I first thought."

"It's nothing." Damon scowled again. "I don't see why they won't let me go back to Kasmara."

"I'm sure they'd like nothing better. I must have stumbled over five of your men as I came down the hall." Damita's lips were still twitching. "Good Lord, *kadins*!"

"I told you it wasn't my idea." There was suddenly a twinkle in Damon's eyes. "I don't like candy, and my room was full of flowers. My chieftains didn't know what else to give me to make me happy while I was here."

"Which, of course, is of paramount importance."

"Of course," Damon agreed. Then the smile faded from his lips. "To everyone but Cam. Since he's not with you, I take it he's still angry with me."

Damita hesitated before nodding. "He wouldn't come with me. I've never seen him so upset."

"It's not surprising." Damon's finger began tracing diamond patterns on the sheet. "I risked your life. I'd probably feel the same way if I were he."

"But you could have died trying to save us," Damita said gently. "You were very brave, Damon."

"My men should have searched the terminal more thoroughly. If anyone had to pay for my mistake, it shouldn't have been you or Cam."

"You weren't responsible for your men's mistake."

"Yes, I was." His gaze lifted, and she was shocked at the bleakness in his eyes. "I make the decisions for the El Zabor. God help me, to them I *am* the El Zabor."

"Do you have to be?" Damita asked tentatively.

"Yes." The answer was unequivocal. "They're impossible, unruly children, but they're *my* children."

Possession. Damita remembered Cam saying possession was one of Damon's most dominant characteristics.

Suddenly the weariness was gone from Damon's expression and he was smiling at her. "And I shouldn't complain. I'm impossible too."

Damita smiled back at him. "Yes, you are." She turned to go. "I'd better leave before that nurse comes back with the orderly. I'll tell Cam you're doing well."

A flicker of pain crossed his face. "If you think he'd be interested."

Damita felt a surge of sympathy. There was something very vulnerable about Damon at this moment. "I'm sure he is."

"I'm not so certain. Perhaps he's written me off his list. Heaven knows, it's about time. He's been short-changed in our friendship since we were boys together." He smiled crookedly. "Thanks for coming, Damita."

"I'll be back tomorrow." She paused. "By the way, you wouldn't happen to know what happened to Belstrop? He seems to have mysteriously disappeared before the police arrived at the airport."

Damon's lids quickly hooded his eyes. "How should I know? I was unconscious until I arrived at the hospital."

"I realize that." Damita grimaced. "Your men were all over the place. They made such a commotion when they found out you were shot, I'm surprised they didn't try to keep the ambulance from taking you."

"As I said, to them I represent the El Zabor."

"It's not only that. They love you."

He gave a half shrug and didn't answer.

She hesitated, gazing at him with a frown. "I really wish we knew what happened to Belstrop. The authorities are afraid to let Lola out of protective custody."

Damon gazed at her with no expression.

She sighed and turned away.

"Damita."

She stopped and glanced inquiringly over her shoulder.

"Tell Lola to ignore the authorities. She's in no danger."

"You're sure?"

"Belstrop shot me," Damon said simply. "Do you think the El Zabor would just permit him to walk away?"

Damita remembered the almost hysterical grief the sheikh's followers had exhibited before the ambulance attendants had taken him away from them, and a shiver ran down her spine. "No, I guess not." She hurriedly opened the door. "I'll see you tomorrow, Damon."

She quickly walked down the hall past Damon's guards toward the elevator at the end of the hall. Why was she running away? she wondered. Damon wouldn't hurt her. Yet there was something very intimidating about a power as absolute as Damon wielded. Was that why she could sense that terrible loneliness in him? Then the fear was gone as she remembered that moment when she had glimpsed something raw and hurting behind Damon's arrogant facade when he spoke of Cam. Whatever else Damon was, he was also Cam's friend.

The doors of the elevator slid open, and she stepped into the cubicle. Now she had only to convince Cam of that fact, she thought wryly. It wasn't going to prove an easy task. She had never seen Cam so coldly savage about anything. After he had found out that Damon's wound wasn't serious, he had refused to even talk about him. Not that they'd had time to talk about anything else either, she thought wearily. Between all those endless interviews with the local police and the calls from Scotland Yard and Lola, they'd both fallen into bed in total exhaustion for the last two nights. She had expected Cam's anger to abate as time passed, but he had adamantly refused to go with her to the hospital this morning. It was clear something had to be done.

She unconsciously squared her shoulders with a touch of her old belligerence.

And it was obviously being left up to her to do it.

Cam was on the phone and glanced up when Damita walked into the suite at the hotel. "Just a minute," he said into the receiver. "It's Lola." he held out the receiver to Damita. "She wants to talk to you."

"I want to talk to her too." Damita took the receiver. "I've just come from seeing Damon, Lola."

"How is he?" Lola asked. "Has he got all the nurses fetching and carrying as befits his consequence?"

"Well, he's definitely getting a reaction from them," Damita said dryly. "I think one of them is ready to slip arsenic into his medicine. She's obviously not accustomed to men who challenge her authority."

Lola laughed. "None of us are until we run across Damon."

"He gave me a message for you." Damita paused. "He told me to tell you to ignore what Scotland Yard says and go your merry way. You're safe from Belstrop."

There was a silence on the other end of the line. "Thank heaven," Lola said finally. "I didn't realize what a weight I was dragging around until you just broke the chain. He's sure?"

"I don't think there's any question that Belstrop is permanently out of the picture."

"I feel as if I can float away into the stratosphere." Lola's voice was lilting. "I think I'll go shopping to celebrate. . . ."

Damita laughed. "Paris?"

"No, I was thinking more on the lines of Princeton or maybe Stanford. Perhaps I'll pick up a degree or two to suit my new image. It's about time I concentrated on what I put in my head instead of on my body. Who knows? I might even decide on a career."

"Who knows?" Damita echoed. "Are we going to see you before you start on this academic binge?"

"Of course, I'm going to fly to Sydney as soon as I tear myself away from these lovely gentlemen here at Scotland Yard. Is all well with you, *querida*?"

"Yes," Damita said softly. "But there are some things I want to talk to you about," she paused. "I love you, Lola."

"I love you too." Lola's voice was a little husky. "I think I'd better hang up now. It's going to take me forever to convince these detectives I'm going to leave whether they like it or not. I'll see you in a few days, Damita." She paused. "Is there something wrong with Cam? He sounded . . . strained."

"He is." Damita's hand tightened on the receiver. "But I intend to put that straight right away. Good-bye, Lola." She broke the connection.

"Damon got rid of Belstrop?" Cam asked from behind her.

She turned to face him. "I don't think Damon had anything to do with it," she said. "He wouldn't tell me what happened, but I think he was protecting some of his followers. You saw how they reacted when they realized he was hurt."

Cam nodded curtly. "Who could miss it? They went crazy."

"They love him." She added softly, "Just as you do."

Cam turned abruptly away. "I've ordered lunch. I thought we'd eat and then take a launch trip around the harbor. You need to unwind after all you've been through these last few days."

"You're the one who needs to unwind," Damita said. "Even Lola noticed you sounded strained."

"Then maybe the trip will do me good too."

"I don't think that's the remedy." Damita hesitated, and then said quickly, "Go see Damon, Cam."

"I don't want to talk about Damon." Cam moved toward the doors of the terrace. "It's warm out today. Would you like to eat on the terrace?"

"No, I don't want to eat on the terrace." Damita gazed at him in exasperation. "I want to talk about Damon. Now, stop being stubborn and let's bring it out in the open."

"This isn't your concern, Damita."

"The hell it isn't. I think it's very much my concern. You're so uptight you're ready to explode, and Damon is terribly unhappy."

"I don't give a damn how Damon feels."

"I know that isn't true. I could see how close you were. Why don't—"

"No." Cam whirled to face her. "Why are you so worried about Damon? He almost got you *killed*. When I heard that shot . . ." He closed his eyes. "Oh, dear God, I was scared."

"Cam . . ." She crossed the distance between them and slipped into his arms. "I was scared too. It was a terrible time, but it's over now."

His arms closed around her with viselike force. "Not for me. I don't think it will ever be over. When I saw Belstrop pointing that gun at you . . ." His grip tightened. "And then you kept *arguing* with him. If Belstrop didn't murder you, I was tempted to do it myself for scaring me like that."

"Well, he had no need to take you. It didn't make sense."

"Hush. Don't talk about it anymore." He laughed mirthlessly. "Look at me. I'm shaking just thinking about it."

Damita nestled closer as she experienced a rush of protective tenderness. She'd had no idea Cam had been so affected by the episode with Belstrop. For her it had been a terrible nightmare but one that was already fading.

But Cam was reacting much differently. "Cam, I have to talk about it. I love you and—"

"You do?" He pushed her away to look down at her. "That's the first time you've told me you love me."

She made a face. "And it had to be now in the middle of a disagreement. As usual, my timing is terrible."

"There's no bad timing for an admission like that," Cam said softly. "Say it again."

She met his gaze. "I love you, Cam." She stood on tiptoe and kissed him gently on the lips. "I'll love you forever and ever and ever."

"Hallelujah." A radiant smile lit his face. "I think this deserves a celebration."

"You too?" Damita smiled up at him. "Lola's going to celebrate by going on a college-shopping spree. What did you have in mind?"

Cam cradled her face in his two hands. "A wedding."

She went still. "Now?"

"Now." Cam was gazing down at her with love and a touch of wistfulness. "I want to say the vows, Damita, and I want to hear you say them. It's important to me."

Yes, she knew the rituals would be important to Cam. Shining promises that would last through the rest of their lives.

"It's important to me too," she said huskily. "And I can't think of a better way to celebrate."

He gave her a quick, hard kiss. "Good. I'll make a few calls and see if I can cut through some of the red tape." His hands dropped from her face and he turned away. "Maybe we'll be able to substitute a wedding for that harbor cruise this afternoon."

"Not this afternoon, Cam." Then, when she saw his disappointed expression, she rushed on. "I want Lola to be at my wedding. She said that she'd be here in a few days."

He nodded understandingly. "Okay, we'll wait. It will give me time to get my brother, Jordan, and his wife here from San Francisco. But they'd all better be prepared to be whisked off to the chapel as soon as their planes touch down."

"Perhaps not quite that soon," Damita said firmly, "because I want Damon there too."

"No." Cam moved forward with a frown. "I told you—"

"I know what you told me." Damita's jaw squared determinedly. "But I'll be damned if I let you give me a guilt trip for the rest of my life."

"Guilt trip? No one's giving you a guilt trip."

"What else do you call it? You and Damon have been friends since you were children. You love each other. Now I suddenly appear on the scene and ruin everything."

"You're not to blame for what happened." Cam's lips twisted. "Damon knew how important you were to me and he still put you at risk."

"And stopped a bullet trying to negate that risk."

"It doesn't matter. He used you for his own ends." Cam's hands clenched into fists at his sides. "I almost lost you. Do you think I can forgive him that?"

She took a step closer. "So Damon made a mistake. You told me yourself that his values aren't the same as yours. He's difficult and arrogant and as changeable as quicksilver."

His lips twisted. "You seem to have him down pat. You haven't described a very charming individual. Why are you defending him?"

She smiled faintly. "Because I think I finally understand him, and because I'm probably as difficult as he is." She held up her hand as he started to protest. "I'm trying to do better, but I still have those thorns and I'll probably still have them when I am a little gray-haired old lady. You say you don't mind my faults. Why can't you accept Damon's?"

"I can accept them. Except where you're—" He stopped.

"Except where I'm concerned?" she finished. "Because you love me?"

"Because I love you," he said hoarsely. "You're the best and brightest thing that's ever come into my life. He had no right to make me run the risk of losing you."

Damita swallowed to ease the tightness of her throat. "I'm glad you feel that way about me." She smiled tremulously. "Even though it proves the old adage that love is blind." Suddenly her eyes widened as something startling occurred to her. "Or perhaps it's not blind. Perhaps you need me to be as difficult as I am, just as you need Damon to be as difficult as he is."

"You're not making sense."

"Yes, I am." She took a step closer, her gaze

meeting his with a sudden urgency. "I've just realized something. You're one of the golden people, Cam. The port in the storm, the protector, the peacemaker. People like Lola, Damon, and I are so desperate for the life preserver you throw out to us that we just grab it and hold on. We never stop to think that maybe you had no choice but to throw it. It's your nature and the only way you can be fulfilled. You liked helping Damon at school, didn't you?"

"Well, it was certainly a challenge," he said dryly.

"No, you really *liked* it. It satisfied you, didn't it?"

"I guess it did," he said slowly. "I never thought about it."

"And Lola and you were friends but you never became involved until she needed you." She grimaced. "And heaven knows I needed you to rip out all those bramble bushes I'd planted." She smiled at him with sudden brilliance. "Lord, I'm relieved."

"Relieved?" Cam asked, puzzled.

She nodded vigorously. "You have no idea what a burden it is for someone like me to love someone like you. You're so blasted nice, I was afraid I'd spend the rest of my life being humbly grateful for having you love me."

Cam's lips twisted. "You, humble?"

"Well, niceness on the scale of yours does intimidate me." She threw her arms around him and hugged him with all her strength. "But now I don't have to worry. You need me."

"I thought you knew," he said gently. "It's all a part of loving."

"No, you really *need* me to complete you. Isn't that wonderful?"

"Yes." He gazed bemusedly down into her glowing face. "I guess it is wonderful."

"And you need Damon too." He glared at her and she gave him a little shake. "You do. The same way you need me."

A faint smile tugged at his lips. "There are differences, as Damon would be the first to acknowledge."

"You know what I mean. You like dealing with the problems Damon creates. If you'd been there this morning, you would have enjoyed the hell out of straightening out the weird mess with the head nurse and the *kadins.*"

"*Kadins?* At the hospital?"

"Two of them. And there may be a major brouhaha about Damon's guards in the hall. Damon threatened to have the nurse carried out and . . ." She trailed off and smiled with satisfaction.

Cam was swearing softly under his breath. "My God, he's been there only two days. Give him another day and they'll probably pull the plug on him."

"They've only got him hooked to an IV. It's not as if they could shut off his life support system. Of course, he did say something about yelling for his guards when the head nurse gives him his next shot."

"Don't tell me any more." Cam groaned. In two strides he was at the phone, lifting the receiver. "What's his room number? If Damon's called on his guards, we'll be lucky if the hospital is still standing."

"Why don't we go see?" she asked softly. "Visiting hours aren't over until three."

He slowly put the receiver back onto the cradle and stood looking at her. A faint smile touched his lips. "You're a very manipulative lady."

She shook her head. "Only when it's for your own good. And Damon is good for you, just as I am."

"I guess this means we don't go for our cruise?"

"I get seasick anyway. And you'll enjoy this more."

"But will you?"

"Oh, yes." She smiled at him lovingly across the room. Happiness lay like a sunlit veil over the entire world. Shining promises and secret gardens and now the knowledge that she was as necessary to Cam as he was to her. "Oh, yes, I'll enjoy it, love."

THE EDITOR'S CORNER

A critic once wrote that LOVESWEPT books have "the most off-the-wall titles" of any romance line. And recently, I got a letter from a reader asking me who is responsible for the "unusual titles" of our books. (Our fans are so polite; I'll bet she wanted to substitute "strange" for unusual!) Whether off-the-wall or unusual—I prefer to think of them as memorable—our titles are dreamed up by authors as well as editors. (We editors must take the responsibility for the most outrageous titles, though.) Next month you can look forward to six wonderful LOVESWEPTs that are as original, strong, amusing—yes, even as off-the-wall—as their titles.

First, **McKNIGHT IN SHINING ARMOR,** LOVESWEPT #276, by Tami Hoag, is an utterly heartwarming story of a young divorced woman, Kelsie Connors, who has two children to raise while holding down two *very* unusual jobs. She's trying to be the complete Superwoman when she meets hero Alec McKnight. Their first encounter, while hilarious, holds the potential for disaster . . . as black lace lingerie flies through the air of the conservative advertising executive's office. But Alec is enchanted, not enraged—and then Kelsie has to wonder if the "disaster" isn't what he's done to her heart. A joyous reading experience.

SHOWDOWN AT LIZARD ROCK, LOVESWEPT #277, by Sandra Chastain, features one of the most gorgeous and exciting pairs of lovers ever. Kaylyn Smith has the body of Wonder Woman and the face of Helen of Troy, and handsome hunk King Vandergriff realizes the

(continued)

moment he sets eyes on her that he's met his match. She is standing on top of Lizard Rock, protesting his construction company's building of a private club on the town's landmark. King just climbs right up there and carries her down . . . but she doesn't surrender. (Well, not immediately.) You'll delight in the feisty shenanigans of this marvelous couple.

CALIFORNIA ROYALE, LOVESWEPT #278, by Deborah Smith, is one of the most heart-stoppingly beautiful of love stories. Shea Somerton is elegant and glamorous just like the resort she runs; Duke Araiza is sexy and fast just like the Thoroughbreds he raises and trains. Both have heartbreaking pain in their pasts. And each has the fire and the understanding that the other needs. But their goals put them at cross-purposes, and neither of them can bend . . . until a shadow from Shea's early days falls over their lives. A thrilling romance.

Get out the box of tissues when you settle down to enjoy **WINTER'S DAUGHTER**, LOVESWEPT #279, by Kathleen Creighton, because you're bound to get a good laugh and a good cry from this marvelous love story. Tannis Winter, disguised as a bag-lady, has gone out onto the streets to learn about the plight of the homeless and to search for cures for their ills. But so has town councilman Dillon James, a "derelict" with mysterious attractions for the unknowing Tannis. Dillon is instantly bewitched by her courage and compassion . . . by the scent of summer on her skin and the brilliance of winter in her eyes. Their hunger for each other grows quickly . . . and to ravenous proportions. Only a risky confrontation can clear up the misunderstandings they face, so that they can finally have it all. We think you're going to treasure this very rich and very dramatic love story.

Completing the celebration of her fifth year as a published writer, the originator of continuing character romances, Iris Johansen, gives us the breathlessly emotional love story of the Sheik you met this month, exciting Damon El Karim, in **STRONG, HOT WINDS**, LOVESWEPT #280. Damon has vowed to punish the lovely Cory Brandel, the mother of his son, whom she's kept secret from him. To do so, he has her kidnapped with the

(continued)

boy and brought to Kasmara. But in his desert palace, as they set each other off, his sense of barbaric justice and her fury at his betrayal quickly turn into quite different emotions. Bewildered by the tenderness and the wild need he feels for her, Damon fears he can never have Cory's love. But at last, Cory has begun to understand what makes this complex and charismatic man tick—and she fears she isn't strong enough to give him the enduring love he so much deserves! Crème de la crème from Iris Johansen. I'm sure you join all of us at Bantam in wishing her not five, but *fifty* more years of creating great love stories!

Closing out the month in a very big way is **PARADISE CAFE**, LOVESWEPT #281, by Adrienne Staff. And what a magnificent tale this is. Beautiful Abby Clarke is rescued by ruggedly handsome outdoorsman Jack Gallagher—a man of few words and fast moves, especially when trying to haul in the lady whom destiny has put in his path. But Abby is not a risk taker. She's an earnest, hardworking young woman who's always put her family first . . . but Jack is an impossible man to walk away from with his sweet, wild passion that makes her yearn to forget about being safe. And Jack is definitely *not* safe for Abby . . . he's a man with wandering feet. You'll relish the way the stay-at-home and the vagabond find that each has a home in the center of the other's heart. A true delight.

I trust that you'll agree with me that the six LOVE-SWEPTs next month are as memorable as their off-the-wall titles!

Enjoy!

Carolyn Nichols

Carolyn Nichols
   Editor
LOVESWEPT
Bantam Books
666 Fifth Avenue
New York, NY 10103

THE HOMETOWN HUNK CONTEST

FOR EVERY WOMAN WHO HAS EVER SAID—
"I know a man who looks
just like the hero of this book"
—HAVE WE GOT A CONTEST FOR YOU!

To help celebrate our fifth year of publishing LOVESWEPT we are having a fabulous, fun-filled event called THE HOMETOWN HUNK contest. We are going to reissue six classic early titles by six of your favorite authors.

DARLING OBSTACLES by Barbara Boswell
IN A CLASS BY ITSELF by Sandra Brown
C.J.'S FATE by Kay Hooper
THE LADY AND THE UNICORN by Iris Johansen
CHARADE by Joan Elliott Pickart
FOR THE LOVE OF SAMI by Fayrene Preston

Here, as in the backs of all July, August, and September 1988 LOVESWEPTS you will find "cover notes" just like the ones we prepare at Bantam as the background for our art director to create our covers. These notes will describe the hero and heroine, give a teaser on the plot, and suggest a scene for the cover. Your part in the contest will be to see if a great looking local man—or men, if your hometown is so blessed—fits our description of one of the heroes of the six books we will reissue.

THE HOMETOWN HUNK who is selected (one for each of the six titles) will be flown to New York via United Airlines and will stay at the Loews Summit Hotel—the ideal hotel for business or pleasure in midtown Manhattan—for two nights. All travel arrangements made by Reliable Travel International, Incorporated. He will be the model for the new cover of the book which will be released in mid-1989. The six people who send in the winning photos of their HOMETOWN HUNK will receive a pre-selected assortment of LOVESWEPT books free for one year. Please see the Official Rules above the Official Entry Form for full details and restrictions.

We can't wait to start judging those pictures! Oh, and you must let the man you've chosen know that you're entering him in the contest. After all, if he wins he'll have to come to New York.

Have fun. Here's your chance to get the cover-lover of your dreams!

Carolyn Nichols

Carolyn Nichols
Editor
LOVESWEPT
Bantam Books
666 Fifth Avenue
New York, NY 10102–0023

THE HOMETOWN HUNK CONTEST

DARLING OBSTACLES
(Originally Published as LOVESWEPT #95)
By Barbara Boswell

COVER NOTES

The Characters:

Hero:
GREG WILDER's gorgeous body and "to-die-for" good looks haven't hurt him in the dating department, but when most women discover he's a widower with four kids, they head for the hills! Greg has the hard, muscular build of an athlete, and his light brown hair, which he wears neatly parted on the side, is streaked blond by the sun. Add to that his aquamarine blue eyes that sparkle when he laughs, and his sensual mouth and generous lower lip, and you're probably wondering what woman in her right mind wouldn't want Greg's strong, capable surgeon's hands working their magic on her—kids or no kids!

Personality Traits:
An acclaimed neurosurgeon, Greg Wilder is a celebrity of sorts in the planned community of Woodland, Maryland. Authoritative, debonair, self-confident, his reputation for engaging in one casual relationship after another almost overshadows his prowess as a doctor. In reality, Greg dates more out of necessity than anything else, since he has to attend one social function after another. He considers most of the events boring and wishes he could spend more time with his children. But his profession is a difficult and demanding one—and being both father and mother to four kids isn't any less so. A thoughtful, generous, sometimes befuddled father, Greg tries to do it all. Cerebral, he uses his intellect and skill rather than physical strength to win his victories. However, he never expected to come up against one Mary Magdalene May!

Heroine:
MARY MAGDALENE MAY, called Maggie by her friends, is the thirty-two-year-old mother of three children. She has shoulder-length auburn hair, and green eyes that shout her Irish heritage. With high cheekbones and an upturned nose covered with a smattering of freckles, Maggie thinks of herself more as the girl-next-door type. Certainly, she believes, she could never be one of Greg Wilder's beautiful escorts.

Setting: The small town of Woodland, Maryland

The Story:
Surgeon Greg Wilder wanted to court the feisty and beautiful widow who'd been caring for his four kids, but she just wouldn't let him past her doorstep! Sure that his interest was only casual, and that he preferred more sophisticated women, Maggie May vowed to keep Greg at arm's length. But he wouldn't take no for an answer. And once he'd crashed through her defenses and pulled her into his arms, he was tireless—and reckless—in his campaign to win her over. Maggie had found it tough enough to resist one determined doctor; now he threatened to call in his kids and hers as reinforcements—seven rowdy snags to romance!

Cover scene:
As if romancing Maggie weren't hard enough, Greg can't seem to find time to spend with her without their children around. Stealing a private moment on the stairs in Maggie's house, Greg and Maggie embrace. She is standing one step above him, but she still has to look up at him to see into his eyes. Greg's hands are on her hips, and her hands are resting on his shoulders. Maggie is wearing a very sheer, short pink nightgown, and Greg has on wheat-colored jeans and a navy and yellow striped rugby shirt. Do they have time to kiss?

THE HOMETOWN HUNK CONTEST

IN A CLASS BY ITSELF
(Originally Published as LOVESWEPT #66)
By Sandra Brown

COVER NOTES

The Characters:

Hero:
LOGAN WEBSTER would have no trouble posing for a
Scandinavian travel poster. His wheat-colored hair always
seems to be tousled, defying attempts to control it, and
falls across his wide forehead. Thick eyebrows one shade
darker than his hair accentuate his crystal blue eyes. He
has a slender nose that flairs slightly over a mouth that
testifies to both sensitivity and strength. The faint lines
around his eyes and alongside his mouth give the impression that reaching the ripe age of 30 wasn't all fun and
games for him. Logan's square, determined jaw is punctu-
ated by a vertical cleft. His broad shoulders and narrow
waist add to his tall, lean appearance.

Personality traits:
Logan Webster has had to scrape and save and fight for
everything he's gotten. Born into a poor farm family, he
was driven to succeed and overcome his "wrong side of
the tracks" image. His businesses include cattle, real estate, and natural gas. Now a pillar of the community,
Logan's life has been a true rags-to-riches story. Only
Sandra Brown's own words can describe why he is masculinity epitomized: "Logan had 'the walk,' that saddle-
tramp saunter that was inherent to native Texan men,
passed down through generations of cowboys. It was, without even trying to be, sexy. The unconscious roll of the
hips, the slow strut, the flexed knees, the slouching stance,
the deceptive laziness that hid a latent aggressiveness."
Wow! And not only does he have "the walk," but he's fun

and generous and kind. Even with his wealth, he feels at home living in his small hometown with simple, hard-working, middle-class, backbone-of-America folks. A born leader, people automatically gravitate toward him.

Heroine:
DANI QUINN is a sophisticated twenty-eight-year-old woman. Dainty, her body compact, she is utterly feminine. Dani's pale, lustrous hair is moonlight and honey spun together, and because it is very straight, she usually wears it in a chignon. With golden eyes to match her golden hair, Dani is the one woman Logan hasn't been able to get off his mind for the ten years they've been apart.

Setting: Primarily on Logan's ranch in East Texas.

The Story:
Ten years had passed since Dani Quinn had graduated from high school in the small Texas town, ten years since the night her elopement with Logan Webster had ended in disaster. Now Dani approached her tenth reunion with uncertainty. Logan would be there . . . Logan, the only man who'd ever made her shiver with desire and need, but would she have the courage to face the fury in his eyes? She couldn't defend herself against his anger and hurt—to do so would demand she reveal the secret sorrow she shared with no one. Logan's touch had made her his so long ago. Could he reach past the pain to make her his for all time?

Cover Scene:
It's sunset, and Logan and Dani are standing beside the swimming pool on his ranch, embracing. The pool is surrounded by semitropical plants and lush flower beds. In the distance, acres of rolling pasture land resembling a green lake undulate into dense, piney woods. Dani is wearing a strapless, peacock blue bikini and sandals with leather ties that wrap around her ankles. Her hair is straight and loose, falling to the middle of her back. Logan has on a light-colored pair of corduroy shorts and a short-sleeved designer knit shirt in a pale shade of yellow.

THE HOMETOWN HUNK CONTEST

C.J.'S FATE
(Originally Published as LOVESWEPT #32)
By Kay Hooper

COVER NOTES

The Characters:

Hero:
FATE WESTON easily could have walked straight off an
Indian reservation. His raven black hair and strong, well-
molded features testify to his heritage. But somewhere
along the line genetics threw Fate a curve—his eyes are
the deepest, darkest blue imaginable! Above those blue
eyes are dark slanted eyebrows, and fanning out from
those eyes are faint laugh lines—the only sign of the fact
that he's thirty-four years old. Tall, Fate moves with easy,
loose-limbed grace. Although he isn't an athlete, Fate takes
very good care of himself, and it shows in his strong
physique. Striking at first glance and fascinating with
each succeeding glance, the serious expressions on his
face make him look older than his years, but with one
smile he looks boyish again.

Personality traits:
Fate possesses a keen sense of humor. His heavy-lidded,
intelligent eyes are capable of concealment, but there is a
shrewdness in them that reveals the man hadn't needed
college or a law degree to be considered intelligent. The set
of his head tells you that he is proud—perhaps even a bit
arrogant. He is attractive and perfectly well aware of that
fact. Unconventional, paradoxical, tender, silly, lusty, gentle, comical, serious, absurd, and endearing are all words
that come to mind when you think of Fate. He is not
ashamed to be everything a man can be. A defense attorney by profession, one can detect a bit of frustrated actor
in his character. More than anything else, though, it's the

impression of humor about him—reinforced by the elusive dimple in his cheek—that makes Fate Weston a scrumptious hero!

Heroine:
C.J. ADAMS is a twenty-six-year-old research librarian. Unaware of her own attractiveness, C.J. tends to play down her pixylike figure and tawny gold eyes. But once she meets Fate, she no longer feels that her short, burnished copper curls and the sprinkling of freckles on her nose make her unappealing. He brings out the vixen in her, and changes the smart, bookish woman who professed to have no interest in men into the beautiful, sexy woman she really was all along. Now, if only he could get her to tell him what C.J. stands for!

Setting: Ski lodge in Aspen, Colorado

The Story:
C.J. Adams had been teased enough about her seeming lack of interest in the opposite sex. On a ski trip with her five best friends, she impulsively embraced a handsome stranger, pretending they were secret lovers—and the delighted lawyer who joined in her impetuous charade seized the moment to deepen the kiss. Astonished at his reaction, C.J. tried to nip their romance in the bud—but found herself nipping at his neck instead! She had met her match in a man who could answer her witty remarks with clever ripostes of his own, and a lover whose caresses aroused in her a passionate need she'd never suspected that she could feel. Had destiny somehow tossed them together?

Cover Scene:
C.J. and Fate virtually have the ski slopes to themselves early one morning, and they take advantage of it! Frolicking in a snow drift, Fate is covering C.J. with snow—and kisses! They are flushed from the cold weather and from the excitement of being in love. C.J. is wearing a sky-blue, one-piece, tight-fitting ski outfit that zips down the front. Fate is wearing a navy blue parka and matching ski pants.

THE HOMETOWN HUNK CONTEST

THE LADY AND THE UNICORN
(Originally Published as LOVESWEPT #29)
By Iris Johansen

COVER NOTES

The Characters:

Hero:
Not classically handsome, RAFE SANTINE's blunt, craggy
features reinforce the quality of overpowering virility about
him. He has wide, Slavic cheekbones and a bold, thrusting chin, which give the impression of strength and authority. Thick black eyebrows are set over piercing dark
eyes. He wears his heavy, dark hair long. His large frame
measures in at almost six feet four inches, and it's hard to
believe that a man with such brawny shoulders and strong
thighs could exhibit the pantherlike grace which charac-
terizes Rafe's movements. Rafe Santine is definitely a man
to be reckoned with, and heroine Janna Cannon does just
that!

Personality traits:
Our hero is a man who radiates an aura of power and
danger, and women find him intriguing and irresistible.
Rafe Santine is a self-made billionaire at the age of thirty-
eight. Almost entirely self-educated, he left school at six-
teen to work on his first construction job, and by the time
he was twenty-three, he owned the company. From there
he branched out into real estate, computers, and oil. Rafe
reportedly changes mistresses as often as he changes shirts.
His reputation for ruthless brilliance has been earned over
years of fighting to the top of the economic ladder from
the slums of New York. His gruff manner and hard personality hide the tender, vulnerable side of him. Rafe also
possesses an insatiable thirst for knowledge that is a
passion with him. Oddly enough, he has a wry sense of

humor that surfaces unexpectedly from time to time. And, though cynical to the extreme, he never lets his natural skepticism interfere with his innate sense of justice.

Heroine:
JANNA CANNON, a game warden for a small wildlife preserve, is a very dedicated lady. She is tall at five feet nine inches and carries herself in a stately way. Her long hair is dark brown and is usually twisted into a single thick braid in back. Of course, Rafe never lets her keep her hair braided when they make love! Janna is one quarter Cherokee Indian by heritage, and she possesses the dark eyes and skin of her ancestors.

Setting: Rafe's estate in Carmel, California

The Story:
Janna Cannon scaled the high walls of Rafe Santine's private estate, afraid of nothing and determined to appeal to the powerful man who could save her beloved animal preserve. She bewitched his guard dogs, then cast a spell of enchantment over him as well. Janna's profound grace, her caring nature, made the tough and proud Rafe grow mercurial in her presence. She offered him a gift he'd never risked reaching out for before—but could he trust his own emotions enough to open himself to her love?

Cover Scene:
In the gazebo overlooking the rugged cliffs at the edge of the Pacific Ocean, Rafe and Janna share a passionate moment together. The gazebo is made of redwood and the interior is small and cozy. Scarlet cushions cover the benches, and matching scarlet curtains hang from the eaves, caught back by tasseled sashes to permit the sea breeze to whip through the enclosure. Rafe is wearing black suede pants and a charcoal gray crew-neck sweater. Janna is wearing a safari-style khaki shirt-and-slacks outfit and suede desert boots. They embrace against the breathtaking backdrop of wild, crashing, white-crested waves pounding the rocks and cliffs below.

THE HOMETOWN HUNK CONTEST

CHARADE
(Originally Published as LOVESWEPT #74)
By Joan Elliott Pickart

COVER NOTES

The Characters:

Hero:
The phrase tall, dark, and handsome was coined to describe TENNES WHITNEY. His coal black hair reaches
past his collar in back, and his fathomless steel gray eyes
are framed by the kind of thick, dark lashes that a woman
would kill to have. Darkly tanned, Tennes has a straight
nose and a square chin, with—you guessed it!—a Kirk
Douglas cleft. Tennes oozes masculinity and virility. He's
a handsome son-of-a-gun!

Personality traits:
A shrewd, ruthless business tycoon, Tennes is a man of
strength and principle. He's perfected the art of buying
floundering companies and turning them around finan-
cially, then selling them at a profit. He possesses a sixth
sense about business—in short, he's a winner! But there
are two sides to his personality. Always in cool command,
Tennes, who fears no man or challenge, is rendered emo-
tionally vulnerable when faced with his elderly aunt's ill-
ness. His deep devotion to the woman who raised him
clearly casts him as a warm, compassionate guy—not at
all like the tough-as-nails executive image he presents.
Leave it to heroine Whitney Jordan to discover the real
man behind the complicated enigma.

Heroine:
WHITNEY JORDAN's russet-colored hair floats past her
shoulders in glorious waves. Her emerald green eyes, full
breasts, and long, slender legs—not to mention her peaches-

and-cream complexion—make her eye-poppingly attractive. How can Tennes resist the twenty-six-year-old beauty? And how can Whitney consider becoming serious with him? If their romance flourishes, she may end up being Whitney Whitney!

Setting: Los Angeles, California

The Story:
One moment writer Whitney Jordan was strolling the aisles of McNeil's Department Store, plotting the untimely demise of a soap opera heartthrob; the next, she was nearly knocked over by a real-life stunner who implored her to be his fiancée! The ailing little gray-haired aunt who'd raised him had one final wish, he said—to see her dear nephew Tennes married to the wonderful girl he'd described in his letters . . . only that girl hadn't existed—until now! Tennes promised the masquerade would last only through lunch, but Whitney gave such an inspired performance that Aunt Olive refused to let her go. And what began as a playful romantic deception grew more breathlessly real by the minute. . . .

Cover Scene:
Whitney's living room is bright and cheerful. The gray carpeting and blue sofa with green and blue throw pillows gives the apartment a cool but welcoming appearance. Sitting on the sofa next to Tennes, Whitney is wearing a black crepe dress that is simply cut but stunning. It is cut low over her breasts and held at the shoulders by thin straps. The skirt falls to her knees in soft folds and the bodice is nipped in at the waist with a matching belt. She has on black high heels, but prefers not to wear any jewelry to spoil the simplicity of the dress. Tennes is dressed in a black suit with a white silk shirt and a deep red tie.

THE HOMETOWN HUNK CONTEST

FOR THE LOVE OF SAMI
(Originally Published as LOVESWEPT #34)
By Fayrene Preston

COVER NOTES

Hero:
DANIEL PARKER-ST. JAMES is every woman's dream come true. With glossy black hair and warm, reassuring blue eyes, he makes our heroine melt with just a glance. Daniel's lean face is chiseled into assertive planes. His lips are full and firmly sculptured, and his chin has the determined and arrogant thrust to it only a man who's sure of himself can carry off. Daniel has a lot in common with Clark Kent. Both wear glasses, and when Daniel removes them to make love to Sami, she thinks he really is Superman!

Personality traits:
Daniel Parker-St. James is one of the Twin Cities' most respected attorneys. He's always in the news, either in the society columns with his latest society lady, or on the front page with his headline cases. He's brilliant and takes on only the toughest cases—usually those that involve millions of dollars. Daniel has a reputation for being a deadly opponent in the courtroom. Because he's from a socially prominent family and is a Harvard graduate, it's expected that he'll run for the Senate one day. Distinguished-looking and always distinctively dressed—he's fastidious about his appearance—Daniel gives off an unassailable air of authority and absolute control.

Heroine:
SAMUELINA (SAMI) ADKINSON is secretly a wealthy heiress. No one would guess. She lives in a converted warehouse loft, dresses to suit no one but herself, and dabbles in the creative arts. Sami is twenty-six years old, with

long, honey-colored hair. She wears soft, wispy bangs and has very thick brown lashes framing her golden eyes. Of medium height, Sami has to look up to gaze into Daniel's deep blue eyes.

Setting: St. Paul, Minnesota

The Story:
Unpredictable heiress Sami Adkinson had endeared herself to the most surprising people—from the bag ladies in the park she protected . . . to the mobster who appointed himself her guardian . . . to her exasperated but loving friends. Then Sami was arrested while demonstrating to save baby seals, and it took powerful attorney Daniel Parker-St. James to bail her out. Daniel was smitten, soon cherishing Sami and protecting her from her night fears. Sami reveled in his love—and resisted it too. And holding on to Sami, Daniel discovered, was like trying to hug quicksilver. . . .

Cover Scene:
The interior of Daniel's house is very grand and supremely formal, the decor sophisticated, refined, and quietly tasteful, just like Daniel himself. Rich traditional fabrics cover plush oversized custom sofas and Regency wing chairs. Queen Anne furniture is mixed with Chippendale and is subtly complemented with Oriental accent pieces. In the library, floor-to-ceiling bookcases filled with rare books provide the backdrop for Sami and Daniel's embrace. Sami is wearing a gold satin sheath gown. The dress has a high neckline, but in back is cut provocatively to the waist. Her jewels are exquisite. The necklace is made up of clusters of flowers created by large, flawless diamonds. From every cluster a huge, perfectly matched teardrop emerald hangs. The earrings are composed of an even larger flower cluster, and an equally huge teardrop-shaped emerald hangs from each one. Daniel is wearing a classic, elegant tuxedo.

LOVESWEPT® HOMETOWN HUNK CONTEST

OFFICIAL RULES

> IN A CLASS BY ITSELF by Sandra Brown
> FOR THE LOVE OF SAMI by Fayrene Preston
> C.J.'S FATE by Kay Hooper
> THE LADY AND THE UNICORN by Iris Johansen
> CHARADE by Joan Elliott Pickart
> DARLING OBSTACLES by Barbara Boswell

1. NO PURCHASE NECESSARY. Enter the HOMETOWN HUNK contest by completing the Official Entry Form below and enclosing a sharp color full-length photograph (easy to see details, with the photo being no smaller than 2½″ × 3½″) of the man you think perfectly represents one of the heroes from the above-listed books which are described in the accompanying Loveswept cover notes. Please be sure to fill out the Official Entry Form completely, and also be sure to clearly print on the back of the man's photograph the man's name, address, city, state, zip code, telephone number, date of birth, your name, address, city, state, zip code, telephone number, your relationship, if any, to the man (e.g. wife, girlfriend) as well as the title of the Loveswept book for which you are entering the man. If you do not have an Official Entry Form, you can print all of the required information on a 3″ × 5″ card and attach it to the photograph with all the necessary information printed on the back of the photograph as well. YOUR HERO MUST SIGN BOTH THE BACK OF THE OFFICIAL ENTRY FORM (OR 3″ × 5″ CARD) AND THE PHOTOGRAPH TO SIGNIFY HIS CONSENT TO BEING ENTERED IN THE CONTEST. Completed entries should be sent to:

> BANTAM BOOKS
> HOMETOWN HUNK CONTEST
> Department CN
> 666 Fifth Avenue
> New York, New York 10102-0023

All photographs and entries become the property of Bantam Books and will not be returned under any circumstances.

2. Six men will be chosen by the Loveswept authors as a HOMETOWN HUNK (one HUNK per Loveswept title). By entering the contest, each winner and each person who enters a winner agrees to abide by Bantam Books' rules and to be subject to Bantam Books' eligibility requirements. Each winning HUNK and each person who enters a winner will be required to sign all papers deemed necessary by Bantam Books before receiving any prize. Each winning HUNK will be flown via **United Airlines** from his closest United Airlines-serviced city to New York City and will stay at the ▪ll S⋯r Hotel—the ideal hotel for business or pleasure in midtown Manhattan— for two nights. Winning HUNKS' meals and hotel transfers will be provided by Bantam Books. Travel and hotel arrangements are made by *RELIABLE TRAVEL* and are subject to availability and to Bantam Books' date requirements. Each winning HUNK will pose with a female model at a photographer's studio for a photograph that will serve as the basis of a Loveswept front cover. Each winning HUNK will receive a $150.00 modeling fee. Each winning HUNK will be required to sign an Affidavit of Eligibility and Model's Release supplied by Bantam Books. (Approximate retail value of HOMETOWN HUNK'S PRIZE: $900.00). The six people who send in a winning HOMETOWN HUNK photograph that is used by Bantam will receive free for one year each, LOVESWEPT romance paperback books published by Bantam during that year. (Approximate retail value: $180.00.) Each person who submits a winning photograph

will also be required to sign an Affidavit of Eligibility and Promotional Release supplied by Bantam Books. All winning HUNKS' (as well as the people who submit the winning photographs) names, addresses, biographical data and likenesses may be used by Bantam Books for publicity and promotional purposes without any additional compensation. There will be no prize substitutions or cash equivalents made.

3. All completed entries must be received by Bantam Books no later than September 15, 1988. Bantam Books is not responsible for lost or misdirected entries. The finalists will be selected by Loveswept editors and the six winning HOMETOWN HUNKS will be selected by the six authors of the participating Loveswept books. Winners will be selected on the basis of how closely the judges believe they reflect the descriptions of the books' heroes. Winners will be notified on or about October 31, 1988. If there are insufficient entries or if in the judges' opinions, no entry is suitable or adequately reflects the descriptions of the hero(s) in the book(s), Bantam may decide not to award a prize for the applicable book(s) and may reissue the book(s) at its discretion.

4. The contest is open to residents of the U.S. and Canada, except the Province of Quebec, and is void where prohibited by law. All federal and local regulations apply. Employees of Reliable Travel International, Inc., United Airlines, the Summit Hotel, and the Bantam Doubleday Dell Publishing Group, Inc., their subsidiaries and affiliates, and their immediate families are ineligible to enter.

5. For an extra copy of the Official Rules, the Official Entry Form, and the accompanying Loveswept cover notes, send your request and a self-addressed stamped envelope (Vermont and Washington State residents need not affix postage) before August 20, 1988 to the address listed in Paragraph 1 above.

LOVESWEPT® HOMETOWN HUNK OFFICIAL ENTRY FORM

BANTAM BOOKS
HOMETOWN HUNK CONTEST
Dept. CN
666 Fifth Avenue
New York, New York 10102–0023

HOMETOWN HUNK CONTEST

YOUR NAME_____

YOUR ADDRESS_____

CITY_____ STATE_____ ZIP_____

THE NAME OF THE LOVESWEPT BOOK FOR WHICH YOU ARE ENTERING THIS PHOTO

_____by_____

YOUR RELATIONSHIP TO YOUR HERO_____

YOUR HERO'S NAME_____

YOUR HERO'S ADDRESS_____

CITY_____ STATE_____ ZIP_____

YOUR HERO'S TELEPHONE #_____

YOUR HERO'S DATE OF BIRTH_____

YOUR HERO'S SIGNATURE CONSENTING TO HIS PHOTOGRAPH ENTRY

_____